SPLIT

BY MICHAEL FRENCH

SPLIT IMAGE

Michael French

BANTAM BOOKS
NEW YORK · TORONTO · LONDON · SYDNEY · AUCKLAND

SPLIT IMAGE

A Bantam Book / November 1990

The Starfire logo is a registered trademark of Bantam Books, a division
of Bantam Doubleday Dell Publishing Group, Inc. Registered in U.S. Patent
and Trademark Office and elsewhere.

Book design by Richard Oriolo

Library of Congress Cataloging-in-Publication Data

French, Michael, 1944–
    Split image / by Michael French.
        p.   cm.
    Summary: At his mother's death, seventeen-year-old Garrett is invited to live with
his father in Los Angeles, where a lifestyle that at first seems simply mysterious turns
into a nightmare.
    ISBN: 0-553-07021-5
    [1. Fathers and sons—Fiction. 2. Spies—Fiction.]   I. Title.
PZ7.F88905Sp   1990
[Fic]—dc20   90-713
                                                                                                   CIP
                                                                                                    AC

Published simultaneously in the United States and Canada

Bantam Books are published by Bantam Books, a division of Bantam Doubleday Dell
Publishing Group, Inc. Its trademark, consisting of the words "Bantam Books" and the
portrayal of a rooster, is Registered in U.S. Patent and Trademark Office and in other
countries. Marca Registrada. Bantam Books, 666 Fifth Avenue, New York, New York
10103.

PRINTED IN THE UNITED STATES OF AMERICA

BVG   0 9 8 7 6 5 4 3 2 1

To Timothy and Alison,
the two and only

SPLIT IMAGE

1

Garrett Woolsey looked around his bedroom. Emptied of all the furniture, he thought it would look larger. But it seemed all wrong. As he stood in the middle of the planked pine floor, in the room where he'd spent most of his seventeen years—in the only home he'd ever really known—the walls felt like they were closing in.

At the window his eyes focused on the large blue-and-white van squeezed in the gravel drive. Two movers were hefting the last of the furniture. Garrett wondered about the new family who would eventually move in, and who would occupy his room. As he looked around, there was nothing left now to say it was ever his.

"The taxi's waiting—"

The voice of his uncle Monroe floated up the stairs. Garrett marched ahead, his brand-new jeans almost squeaking and his cowboy boots scraping softly against the floor. An oversized suitcase in each strong hand assured him his balance, but on the landing, turning abruptly, he nearly collided with Monroe.

"Want some help with those, Garrett?" Monroe was out

of breath from his ascent. The pear-shaped torso leaned against the railing, and Monroe tucked his thumbs behind his suspenders. This morning, for whatever reason, he had combed his thinning hair straight over his forehead, the way he did when he went to church or to a funeral.

"Thanks, but I can manage," Garrett said in his soft drawl. He studied his uncle awkwardly. "Listen, I appreciate everything you've done. Thanks."

"You're welcome, son, you know that. But what you're doing—is this what you really want?" Monroe's craggy face squinched up. "I don't think it's what your mother would have wanted."

Garrett didn't want to reignite the argument he'd already had a half dozen times. Why wouldn't Monroe give up? "I can't speak for Mom," Garrett said, trying hard to leave things with his uncle on a positive note. "How can you?"

"I just don't see why you won't stay with me in Rainbow. Because of Sis, you and I, we're family, Garrett. I've known you since you were born. You could finish school where you started, not leave your friends. You could go to college in Little Rock. You wouldn't ever have to worry about a summer job because you could help in the store. If that isn't an offer—"

Garrett turned his eyes away. He really did appreciate his uncle's kindness. For the first few weeks after his mom's death he was sure he would stay in Rainbow. But that was before the letter had arrived.

"You think you can sell all the furniture?" Garrett asked, looking for a neutral subject.

"Half of it's antiques. That's my business, isn't it? I'll find a buyer for the car, too, and manage the house rental. I'll send you the money right away. You don't have to worry about money."

"Just put it in my college fund." Garrett never really had had it easy financially, but now he wasn't worried. "My dad will take care of everything in L.A."

"I'll send you the money," Monroe repeated stubbornly as Garrett hoisted his suitcases and started downstairs.

2

"Garrett, be reasonable. You don't even know your father, how he'll treat you, or what he'll do." His uncle dogged his steps. "How can you go live with someone you don't know?"

"You have to define *know*, Monroe. I *remember* my father. He and Mom didn't split up until I was almost seven. He's sent expensive presents every Christmas and remembered my birthday. Can't you know someone from that? You can know someone cares about you. What I don't know about him, I'll learn."

"It just makes me suspicious—Clarence getting in touch with you out of the blue. What's he want?"

"What's he want?" Garrett called over his shoulder when he reached the entry hall. "He wants to spend time with me. It wasn't exactly out of the blue, considering the circumstances. Hey, you talk about family. . . . What's my dad supposed to be?"

"Here's some good advice, Garrett. Blood ties or not, you should never trust a man who can't hold a job, or changes his address every year like it's nothing more than a fresh set of clothes."

The taxi driver honked his horn.

"Monroe, I'm going to miss my plane."

Garrett felt his face warm. Monroe talked about Clarence Murchinson as if he were some misfit. Garrett thought his father had accomplished a lot. He wouldn't brag to Monroe, but he'd always been proud that his father had been to college and graduate school and had a degree in engineering. It was true, he switched jobs often and moved around, but why did Monroe think that was necessarily negative? Clarence Murchinson was a little bit of a mystery, but a pleasant one. Garrett had always been intrigued by the expensive and elegant presents and cards his father sent, sometimes from halfway around the world. If his father didn't keep in touch by phone or write, Garrett figured, a successful engineer was just too busy. Then, two months ago, his father had sent him a letter. He expressed the pain he felt when he heard about Garrett's mother's death, and was sorry to have been out of touch so long. He

3

offered Garrett support—and a change of scenery—Garrett was welcome to come live with his father in Los Angeles.

"All right, all right," Monroe surrendered in the silence as they walked outside together. "If you're really going, Garrett, enjoy yourself. I love you. Always remember that. I loved your mother, and I'm here for you. I don't have any other family. I'm sorry to lose you." His hand squeezed his nephew's shoulder. "And stay out of trouble, you hear?"

Garrett smiled. "Trouble? Monroe, when have I ever been bad?" He accepted his uncle's peace offering, but he could also feel Monroe's sadness. Before he knew it, Garrett was fighting back his own emotions. His uncle was someone he loved. He'd tried to be a father to Garrett all these years—at least in his own way. It hadn't been easy for either of them to put the fatal car accident behind them.

"I'll call you when I get to L.A. And don't worry, you haven't lost me!" Garrett promised, with a quick grin. He pushed his suitcases into the trunk of the waiting taxi.

"Here, don't forget your book," Monroe said, thrusting a thick paperback into his nephew's hand. "Let's go Europe." he read, head half cocked. "You really going to get there, too? L.A. isn't far enough from Rainbow?"

"Sure gonna try," he said. Garrett knew it had to sound amusing to Monroe. They'd both never been out of Arkansas. His mother had never wanted to travel much. She said she was happiest staying in one place, but that Garrett would have to decide his future for himself one day. Los Angeles would be a start.

"You've always been the dreamer, son." Monroe slipped ahead to open the taxi door. Garrett swung a glance back to the simple stucco home with the shingled roof and the pair of lopsided pepper trees in front. The property sat alone, two miles from Rainbow, like some lonely beacon. He had never thought of it that way until now.

"Hey, Monroe," he suddenly teased as he turned, "you going to come visit me?"

4

"Me—fly to Los Angeles? Be serious." Monroe's foot pawed the ground before a smile lit the lumpy face. "Only if it's to bring you home," he kidded back.

They gave each other a hug, and Garrett sat back in the taxi.

"You can always change your mind," Monroe whispered, as if to himself, but Garrett knew it was meant for him. Monroe waved as the taxi pulled away.

After a few minutes the fifteen blocks of faded storefronts, cafés, and gas stations rose up on the horizon. Garrett knew the view like he knew the seams on a football. Every store, every owner, every crack in the sidewalk. His mother had kept an old postcard of Rainbow from forty years ago; it was hard to see much change.

Garrett had already said good-bye to his friends, but he waved to some of the old-timers on the street. Did they realize he might never come back? As much as he loved Monroe, Garrett knew he didn't want to live with him and be trapped in Rainbow forever. His uncle had no imagination, no dreams. He was a successful businessman in a small town. What kind of ambition was that? In Rainbow there were no secrets, no surprises; everyone knew everything that happened to you. If Garrett stayed, his future would be as flat and predictable as the landscape. Maybe if Clarence had never invited him to California he wouldn't be thinking this way, but his father *had* sent the invitation, and after a while Garrett hadn't been able to think of anything but leaving. It felt like a chance to escape. He'd never realized he'd felt like a prisoner before.

The reflection of his taxi shimmered in the window of the bus station, and then the town passed behind him. That was why it was called Rainbow—Garrett remembered the joke—because it disappeared so quickly.

He'd gently but firmly refused Monroe's offer to drive him to the airport. It would only have dragged on Monroe's quiet pleas to stay. Now he had a chance to think and feel the anticipation all over. The black-and-white photo of his father that Garrett had always kept by his bed was safely in his jean jacket pocket. He didn't need to take it out. He had memorized every line and curve in the rugged, handsome face. When he reached Los Angeles, Garrett was sure, he would know his father as if they'd never been apart.

2

$\mathbf{G}$arrett was certain that he looked like a freak. In his western shirt and cowboy boots, he strode self-consciously through the crowded airport. He had left Arkansas only four hours ago and ended up in what seemed like a time warp. Los Angeles International Airport was a city in itself, a blur of bars, novelty shops, newspaper stands, and thousands of people smartly dressed. Garrett especially noticed the teenagers, who all seemed to wear expensive clothes and sneakers. In Little Rock and Fayetteville there were fashionable people, too, but here the mix of blacks, Latins, Arabs, Asians . . . he had never anticipated that he'd be landing on what felt like another planet. He tried not to feel overwhelmed.

At the baggage rotunda Garrett milled around with the other passengers. Except for his clothes, maybe he would fit in his new city all right. His symmetrical face had a naturally serious look that made him appear older than seventeen; his black, close-cropped hair was always neat. Though short, he was quick and powerful enough to have started as halfback for his old school. He wondered again what the schools would be like in Los Angeles. Competitive, he was sure, in the classroom and out. He was also certain he could handle his senior year. Grades had never been a problem for him, and over the summer he'd kept in shape so he could play football here.

Garrett glanced at his watch. He had expected his father to meet him at the gate. Was something wrong? He began to worry. He'd sent Clarence his flight number and time of arrival, along with a photo. For all his brave assurances to Monroe, Garrett suddenly wondered if he and his father would be an instantaneous match. Maybe they wouldn't be compatible at all. What if his father didn't care for him? Maybe he'd find something objectional in a boy who was very serious, or too quiet, or ambitious to change his life. What if Garrett found something strange about his father, and Monroe was right? He crossed his arms tightly. He hated being anxious. He hated uncertainty.

"Garrett! Garrett Murchinson!"

He turned with a start. Murchinson was his father's name, but Garrett had never used it. Garrett took in the figure striding rapidly toward him, and tried to focus on the handsome face he thought he knew so well. He did recognize it, but there was something bigger than life, something a photograph couldn't capture. Over six feet, long-legged, and wide in the shoulders, Clarence had thick, wavy hair that was graying in front and a full mustache that was still black. His clear eyes shone with intelligence. His mouth was firm and decisive. He wore simple khaki trousers and a short-sleeved shirt—clothes that Garrett might have picked for himself. Garrett focused on the intense, marble-blue eyes. He had imagined giving his father a hug, at least shaking hands, but he was taking in so many impressions that he couldn't even speak.

"Well, look at you," Clarence Murchinson said. "Aren't you a handsome young man!" He had a natural, infectious

8

smile. His hand jumped out and wrapped around Garrett's like a warm vise. "I wanted to meet you at the plane, but I couldn't find a parking space in this bloody airport!"

"That's okay. I knew you'd make it. I'm glad I'm here, too." The words rushed out from behind his nervous smile. He wondered if they made sense.

"First things first. Call me Clarence, or Dad, or whatever you feel comfortable with, okay?"

"Okay."

"Second, whatever you want or need, just speak up. Anytime, anything at all. For a while things might seem foreign to you, but I'll be here to help, if you need it. You know," he said as he yanked Garrett's luggage off the carousel, "I'm very sorry about Alice. I know she was a great mother—I can't take her place—but I'm happy you made the commitment to come. We're going to have a good time together, I promise."

Garrett wanted to carry his own suitcases, but his father already was running interference through the crowd, moving with authority and confidence as he kept talking. A step behind, Garrett listened attentively as Clarence explained about the local climate, politicians, the mixed population, crime statistics, the price of houses. He struggled to take in the flow of words. There was something so intriguing, but Garrett couldn't quite put his finger on it. Maybe it was just how much energy his father radiated.

In the parking lot he scrutinized his father's old Ford. Mercedeses and Porsches wheeled about them, but Clarence didn't seem to care. As they squeezed onto a crowded freeway, the pall of smog became obvious. Garrett couldn't find even a patch of blue. His eyes started to tear.

"There're more cars in the Los Angeles basin than in the rest of the entire state," Clarence said, reading his mind. "Some people here actually *boast* about that, but it's a marvel we all haven't been asphyxiated by carbon monoxide. If the city keeps mushrooming, it could well die a slow death, though everybody denies it. That's because they're too busy having a good time." He gave Garrett a wink. "It's a crazy city—an asylum run by the inmates. At your age, it'll be nothing but fun; mine— well, sometimes I miss the tranquillity of Arkansas."

Garrett slewed an eye to the cars that zigzagged in and out of their lanes.

"So if it's crazy, why do you live here?" Garrett asked.

"The first law of economics. My job. Actually, I travel so much for my company that the city's just a port of convenience."

"You still work for the same aerospace contractor?" Garrett remembered the note on last year's Christmas card.

"Biggest in the state. Our principal plant's in Long Beach."

"Is that far away?"

"Not so far." He studied Garrett. "You mean you've got a week before school starts and you're interested in seeing the place your old man works? That's at the top of your list?" Clarence grinned. "Why don't we go home, then we can head to Disneyland, or take in a Raiders game."

"Let's go to Long Beach," Garrett answered. He wanted his father to know that what was most important was getting to know him. Why not start where Clarence worked? "I know it's Saturday, but would there be something to see?"

"Maybe," Clarence said. "There's only a skeleton crew on weekends, but basically the plant never closes, even at night. Okay, you win. We'll take a little detour and stop off before we head home."

The air turned salty and pungent as his father navigated the freeway. When they crested a hill dotted with expensive-looking homes, the vista of gray, choppy waters unfolded a mile below. Dark thunderheads massed overhead. Winds whipped the small pleasure craft that steered around larger commercial ships. Garrett fixed his eyes ahead, exhilarated at the sight of a port. So this was the ocean. He would definitely have to come back. He was embarrassed

10

to mention that it was the first time he was seeing the deep blue sea.

A freeway exit led them inland again, winding through a warehouse district. They approached several blocks of large unmarked cement buildings that were like bunkers. Barbed-wire fences circled the gloomy fortresses. There were only a few doors visible, all with security personnel at the thresholds.

"Spooky," Garrett observed, sitting up. "This is how I imagine Fort Knox. What's inside?"

"Mostly aircraft and weapons systems. Some sophisticated computers. A lot of design and engineering plans. Seventy percent of our contracting is with the Defense Department. You need a special security clearance for access to most buildings."

"Is everything classified?" Garrett was impressed but disappointed. There wouldn't be much to see after all. "How long have you had a security clearance?" Whenever he was told that something was off-limits, Garrett wanted to know everything about it.

"I received my first low-level clearance maybe eight years ago," Clarence allowed as they parked near a one-story brick annex. "Over time it was upgraded. Now I have access to any spot in the plant. I'll get you into as many places as possible," he promised. Inside the annex, Garrett was given a visitor's badge, which he pinned to his shirt, and his father clipped on another that bore his photograph.

"This place is a small city," Clarence said. "Five thousand strong. All little cogs in a big wheel, I'm afraid."

Garrett thought his father sounded unhappy for being only a simple foot soldier. He wondered if it was true. Someone as bright as Clarence surely had important responsibilities. Maybe his father was modest by nature, just like he was. His clothes and old car were certainly modest. Garrett's head flicked around. The hangar *was* huge—wide enough to handle a 747. There was a feeling

11

of freedom he liked. Once beyond the initial security checkpoint he saw that he could wander pretty much where he pleased. Approaching an interior metal door, Clarence bent over a built-in speaker and announced his full name. The door slid open, and they passed into a low-ceilinged room with no windows.

"How did you do that?" Garrett looked back as the door closed behind them.

"A computer analyzes my voice. It already has my 'print' stored in its memory. No two voices are alike, same as fingerprints."

They paused at a laboratory with a viewing window where men and women in white smocks hunkered over what looked to Garrett like a large jet engine. A couple of camera tripods were clustered in a corner. Soundproof tiles covered the walls and ceiling.

"What's this?"

"It's where I sometimes work."

"Really? Right here? What do you do?"

Garrett waited for his father to respond, but the silence indicated it was somehow inappropriate to ask. They moved toward a work area with a dozen cubicles, each jammed with several desks and almost as many computer terminals. Clarence's desk was neat and tidy.

"Do you use a PC?" his father asked as Garrett hovered over Clarence's computer.

"Only in school. Mom could never afford one for the house. What kind is yours?"

"A three-eighty-six with twenty-megahertz. Thirty-two-K RAM. Integrated super VGA on the motherboard, forty-four-megabyte, twenty-five-millisecond hard drive . . ."

Garrett whistled. "Would I love one like that—"

"Really?" Clarence gave him a wink.

The ones at his old high school were five years old—no hard drives, only black-and-white monitors, 360K floppy disc. The stone age. He hoped his new school was better equipped.

"You want to see something truly impressive?" Clarence asked.

He followed his father to the next hangar, where Clarence had to speak to a security guard before Garrett was allowed in.

"Wow," whispered Garrett. He was mesmerized by the shiny, black jet fighter with swept-back wings and space-age cockpit. The aircraft was relatively small, low to the ground, like a giant toy—Garrett wanted to reach up and touch it.

"It's beautiful." He kept his voice low, as if they were in a sacred place.

"We call it the X-Forty-four. It's a prototype for the air force. The media already know about it, but we generally don't allow outsiders a terribly close look. A computer virtually runs the aircraft. Except for takeoffs and landings, the pilot is almost expendable. It's magical in other ways, too."

"How? What magic?"

Clarence raised a finger to his lips as they took in the stern glance of someone working on Saturday.

"Do you ever work on that plane?" Garrett asked outside as they headed back to the car.

"I'm not at liberty to say, even to you, son."

"You mean it's all top secret."

"Yes. And the work is very technical. It would probably bore you, anyway."

Garrett dropped his eyes in disappointment. He couldn't help feeling a little hurt at being shut out again. He was intelligent. Maybe Clarence didn't know that. And what Garrett didn't understand at first, he always worked hard to figure out. He would never brag, but he wanted Clarence to know what kind of student he was. Garrett decided he would just have to show him. After all, if he had things to learn about Clarence, didn't his father have things to learn about him?

"All I can really tell you about my job," his father said

sympathetically as they navigated back to the freeway, "is I do a lot of traveling. It's the part of my work I enjoy the most." He glanced at Garrett with fresh concern. "You know, that was my one reservation about asking you to come live here."

Garrett frowned. "Why should your traveling make a difference?"

"Who's going to look after you when I'm away?" he asked.

"Don't worry. I'll be fine. Since Mom died, I've gotten used to being alone. I'm responsible."

Garrett suddenly felt the emptiness that sometimes overwhelmed him. Silence fell over the car. Since his mom's death, it happened a lot, usually without warning. Part of him hated the powerlessness—but another part felt pleasantly insulated by his self-pity. He never cried, but his grief welled up and seized hold of him.

He tilted his head away from his father. Garrett had learned the meaning of responsibility long before his mother had died. He had learned it when his father had moved out. "My little man," his mother began calling him when he was seven or eight. His friends hated doing chores, but Garrett gravitated toward household work and errands. He prided himself in how many things he could accomplish in a day—he even put that responsibility ahead of schoolwork and football. He always wanted to protect and take care of his mother. He would do everything for her and himself. He had tried to replace his father by doing what he would have done around the house.

"Garrett—is something wrong?"

His father's voice pulled him out of his fog. He forced a smile. "Nothing," he answered, looking ahead.

"Were you thinking about Alice, maybe?"

Garrett clucked his tongue absently. He did that sometimes when he was nervous. Maybe his father did understand him. "I think about Mom a lot," he confided.

"I'm sorry. You've been through a lot, Garrett."

"It's okay. I guess I'll get over it."

14

"Of course you will. It's natural to feel vulnerable for a while. Sometimes life deals us terrible blows, but we can't run from them, and I know you don't want to, Garrett. I admire that. I also admire anyone who can look at his setbacks and see them as opportunities for change and growth. There're always bright sides, if we look for them."

"You're right," Garrett said appreciatively.

"Speaking of bright sides, do you have a driver's license?"

Garrett was confused. "Sure."

"Then you can use my car whenever I travel. An out-of-state license should be good for awhile. I can always take a taxi to the airport."

"Really? You're not just saying that?"

"I always say what I mean, Garrett. Treat this city as your oyster. Explore to your heart's content!"

Clarence's mood seemed suddenly buoyant, and it ignited Garrett's spirits. Maybe his father didn't reveal all his secrets from work, but at least he respected Garrett's independence. Garrett would never let anybody down, especially his father.

"Where do you go?" he suddenly asked. "Is that top secret?"

"Not really. Europe. The Orient. The Middle East. South Pacific. I'm what you call a troubleshooter."

"Have you been to Africa?"

"Egypt and Morocco."

Garrett stared ahead. He couldn't believe it. His father had traveled so far from life in Rainbow, Arkansas. He was tempted to ask if he could join Clarence sometime. Maybe it would happen; he wasn't going to force it. For now they had to get to know each other, and Garrett reminded himself his main responsibility was doing well at school.

His head dropped back on the seat as he watched his father's strong, sure hands on the wheel. He noted the steady gaze. The erect posture. Garrett still couldn't believe

15

his first impressions. His father was someone very special. Monroe was wrong to have been so worried, and so was he. Garrett put his apprehensions behind him. He trusted his intuition, and now it told him everything was going to work out fine.

3

A soft rain was falling by the time they reached a narrow corner lot in a residential neighborhood of the San Fernando Valley. Garrett was impressed. The immaculate, bright yellow house with white trim stood out against its more shabby neighbors. The lawn and fruit trees looked equally well cared for, and inside, the two-bedroom home was so neat it seemed almost unlived in. The furnishings were simple and practical. A black upright piano sat against one wall, only a few feet from a small, round dining table. A desk for his father was across the room. There was no television or stereo. The house was only a rental, but Clarence's pride dictated caring for it as if it were his own. Shelves in the living room were filled with books. Garrett suspected that his father had read every one. Wedged on the bottom shelf was an ancient-looking football. It fit snugly in the web of Garrett's hand.

"Where did you get this?"

"High school," Clarence answered as he sat on the couch. "I grew up outside of Chicago. My team won city when I was a senior. Guess who was quarterback?"

"You?"

"Threw thirteen consecutive passes that day. Tied some record. Glory days," he said with an amused shrug, but Garrett thought he heard pride in his father's voice. "You play, too, don't you?" Clarence asked.

"How'd you know?"

"Your build, the way you hold the ball—and the fact it was my sport, too."

"But you weren't around to teach me."

"There's such a thing as the gene pool."

An easy smile came to Garrett. "Did you play in college? I want to."

"I went to Columbia, in New York City. It wasn't much of a sports school, particularly for football. Columbia is academic, and back then, in the sixties, it was also very political. I mostly studied."

"Mom said the sixties were so different, but you didn't get involved in any of the campus demonstrations. She said you'd always liked politics. I thought you were a liberal, just like she was."

"Not at that time. Everyone else was a liberal, or a radical—it was a statement more of fashion than politics. I thought most of the kids were hypocrites. They had no idea of the meaning of responsibility. They wanted to criticize and tear down everything, including the United States government, with no clear concept about what would take its place. I stayed away from the rallies and marches. I got sick of the phoniness. I went in the other direction. I was the only one in my class to volunteer for the draft. Spent a year in Vietnam. Infantry."

Garrett's eyes drifted back to the bookcase. On a top shelf, barely visible, were several framed medals. "Mom only told me you were in the army."

"I wasn't exactly proud of my year in Nam, Garrett. I was an exemplary soldier—a hero, if you count the medals—but I came to realize I'd made a horrible mistake. The corruption of the military and our government was far more intolerable than any student hypocrisy. The bloodshed, the bureaucratic ineptitude, the outright lies—by the time my tour was over, I had become the radical I once detested. Sometimes we take strange journeys in life. . . ."

Clarence stretched as he stood, indicating that the conversation was over. "Here's your room," he said as they crossed the floor. A faded wooden desk and study lamp were in one corner, and across from the bed, a set of unpainted pine drawers. Clarence had nailed a small bulletin board above the bedside table. For privacy there was a lock on the door. The room was simple and practical, just like the rest of the house, just like Garrett's father. A window framed the view of the apple tree in the front yard.

"Close your eyes," Clarence ordered.

"What?"

"Close your eyes."

Garrett did as instructed. He heard Clarence moving something. Then he heard the rustling of cords.

"Okay. You can look—"

Garrett blinked as he took in the computer, color monitor, and laser printer, with a red ribbon tied around each. He walked over for a closer examination. Everything was new, and the brands were expensive.

"Just like mine at work," Clarence explained.

"You didn't have to do this—"

"No, I didn't, but I did. I feel badly for neglecting you, Garrett. I know it's been too many years. I want to make up for it. I want to give you the tools to be the best student you can be. You've got enough power in that PC to run the Pentagon," Clarence quipped. "As for the rest of the room, it's pretty bare, but you can make it come to life with your things."

"Everything's fine, perfect," said Garrett, meaning it. He didn't need a lot of posters on the walls. "Thanks for the computer, really."

"Unpack and make yourself comfortable. I've got to run some errands. The supermarket closes at six. I always eat dinner at seven. That leaves a couple hours for reading or

19

working on projects. I don't believe in television or VCRs or movies."

"I watch a little TV," Garrett admitted. "Sports mostly."

"Can you do without it? The things I value, Garrett, are more intangible. Sometimes I'll go to a sporting event, but usually when I have free time I catch up on my reading or try to have an intelligent conversation. . . ."

Garrett nodded in a noncommittal way. He didn't want his father to think he didn't like intellectual pursuits, too, but here in his free time his priority was to get to know his father and to explore his new city. "Anything I can do to help?" he asked.

"Be a good eater tonight." Clarence winked. "I'm fixing veal niçoise. Cooking is a passion with me."

"Sounds great." Garrett had never heard of veal niçoise, but he was sure he would like it if Clarence did. He turned to the door only to find his father had vanished.

Garrett began unpacking. He knew he didn't like to waste time, though he doubted he could match his father's pace. What Clarence had just told him about Chicago, Columbia University, and Vietnam was fascinating. Garrett knew some of his father's life history. His mother had given him details. His parents met at a political fund-raiser in Little Rock. Alice was still a student, but they'd fallen in love and married. After Garrett was born Clarence taught engineering at the local university. It was the longest job he'd ever held, almost seven years, Garrett's mother said. Frustrated by student indifference and faculty politics, he accepted a position with an aerospace company in Washington State. Garrett's mother didn't want to move. There were problems between them, Garrett learned years later, though at the time he thought everyone was happy. He didn't understand why his father was leaving. Garrett and his mother moved to Rainbow. Alice earned a living working with Monroe in his antiques business. She never said any bad things about her ex-husband. She just explained to Garrett that although he was a talented man, Clarence was such a perfectionist, he was

20

difficult to live with. He expected too much of himself and everyone else.

Garrett finished putting his clothes away, everything neat and orderly, because that's the way he was. It was the small town in him, his mother had liked to say, though Garrett also saw the same traits in his father. Sometimes his mom had said he was like his father—the good parts, she'd always added, laughing. Maybe Clarence was right about the gene pool. On his bedside table Garrett resecured the photo of his father in its frame, and stood it next to the one of his mother. He noticed there weren't any photographs around the house. Garrett didn't put up a picture of Monroe, but he made a mental note to call him the next day. He'd buy some postcards and write to his friends back home, too. Then, shoes off, he stretched out on the bed and shut his eyes. In just a few hours his entire life had changed. It was exhausting and exhilarating at the same time.

When he woke it was dark outside. Music was drifting toward him—he almost saw black octave notes dancing around him. His father's sonorous voice filled the house. He was ashamed to admit he knew almost nothing about opera, but he figured his father was singing some aria. Garrett told himself that music was something he would want to learn about.

4

"We're being taxed to death. There's no middle class left, Garrett. Just rich and poor." His father's disgusted face looked at the traffic in front. "The forces of capitalism have created a two-tier society. Do you think that's what our forefathers imagined for this country?"

In only a week Garrett had gotten used to listening to his father's strong opinions. The morning rush-hour traffic crept. Garrett could feel the butterflies swarming in his stomach. He didn't want to be late for his first day at school. Clarence maneuvered off the freeway to a side road that paralleled blocks of elegant homes and manicured lawns. Los Angeles was like a jigsaw puzzle. Clarence had driven him through Bel Air, Beverly Hills, Holmby Hills, then east Los Angeles, Watts, and other barrios. No two pieces were quite alike, yet some were more alike than others. The contrast between rich and poor here *was* extreme. Garrett had never seen such poverty in Rainbow. He knew people were poor, but Watts was truly horrifying to him.

"Our government gives lip service to democracy, Garrett,

but we're really a country of special interests. The voice of the people? It's mute. The voice of money and power controls our destiny."

The car swung past a "private" sign and down a winding road surrounded by lush landscaping and towering eucalyptuses. Garrett came to attention when they passed through a carved stone entrance and saw the two- and three-story brick buildings that had been concealed from the freeway. An athletic field and gymnasium were in the distance; closer in were an auditorium and amphitheater. The campus was what Garrett imagined a college would be. His father rolled to a stop. Expensive cars, mostly Mercedeses and Porsches, were dropping off boys his age. Some kids drove up and parked themselves.

"This is the local public high school?" Garrett asked, incredulous.

A smile framed Clarence's rugged face. "Hardly. It's Wilshire Academy. The finest boys' day school in this city. I wanted to save this as a surprise. Think of it as an early birthday present. The school's not too shabby athletically, either."

"Wait, wait," said Garrett, confused, "how can you afford this?" He had seen his father's small cubicle at the aerospace company, and Clarence had told him money was not growing on a tree out back. How could he handle a swanky prep school tuition? After what he'd just been saying about the rich. . . .

"I have some money saved," his father answered. "You're important to me, Garrett. And your education is the most important thing of all. I won't waste money on overpriced houses or new cars or foolish gadgets. Consumerism is a disease. It just shows how unhappy people are, losing themselves in objects. But education—honing and stimulating the mind—no price or value can be put on that."

"You really want me here?" He tried to sound casual. The butterflies were on the rampage. For a moment he wished he were back in Rainbow.

"I want the best education for you, son. The fact that the rich want the same thing for their children is immaterial. You have to block out their affectations and focus on what's relevant." He gave Garrett's shoulder a pat. "You're already enrolled, but do you want me to come in and register you?"

"I can do it."

"If you're trying out for the football team, I'll pick you up around six."

"It's okay. Is there a bus to get home?"

His father nodded.

"Then I'll take it."

Garrett wanted to show he could be in charge. Despite his father's offer of assistance, he sensed that Clarence expected independence of him. It was a value they both thought was important.

Garrett waved good-bye and headed toward the administration building. The kids in front of him were dressed virtually alike, as if they all shopped at the same expensive store. A few eyed him back, and he felt self-conscious in his shirt and fat belt buckle. He felt like an Arkansas cowboy surrounded by city slickers. He pushed his self-doubts out of his head and went inside.

His old school had looked like an army barracks, but this place took his breath away. Rows of lockers gleamed like the floors, or the trophy case, which was packed six deep. Paintings, obviously by students, hung on the walls. On a bulletin board were prize essays written in French and German, and photos from students' trips abroad.

A secretary greeted him in the administration office and asked him to fill out papers. He penciled in his class schedule and health information before returning to the top of the page. *Murchinson, Garrett W.*, he wrote on the first line. He and Clarence had never discussed changing his surname. His mother had gone back to using Woolsey. He thought of his mother and wondered what she'd think. She'd want him to be happy. Arkansas was in the past, this was a new life—why not a new identity? The secret

24

felt right. Who at his new school would know any differently? No one was being hurt. He was sure that choosing his father's name would please Clarence. Hadn't he called him Garrett Murchinson at the airport?

A bell sounded as he found his first room. He hunkered down in the back row and darted a glance at the small group of kids. Another bell, and the teacher, tall and willowy, turned to face the flag in the corner. Feet scuffled to attention.

I pledge allegiance
To the flag
Of the United States of America
And to the republic
For which it stands. . . .

His hand over his heart, Garrett recited the words he'd known since kindergarten. He smiled and realized he still believed in these words. Arkansas or L.A., at least some things were the same. When everyone was seated, the teacher approached the blackboard and scrawled the words FRENCH REVOLUTION, 1789–1799.

"For those who don't know me, my name is Mr. Fenton, and this is History 101." Garrett thought the teacher's milky brown eyes blazed right into him. "Without looking at last semester's notes, who would like to tell me the French king who held absolute power in 1789?"

Garrett waited for someone to raise his hand, but the room was as quiet as the wall clock. Was everyone still daydreaming about summer? If Wilshire Academy was an elite school. . . .

"Louis the Sixteenth," Garrett announced in the silence.

He had not meant to be first, but the words had popped out. Heads turned. Mr. Fenton peered over his glasses. "You are?"

"Garrett Murchinson."

"I don't believe we've met."

"No, sir. I'm a transfer. From Arkansas."

The drawl in his speech sounded more self-conscious

suddenly, as if he were holding a megaphone to his lips. The low rumble of laughter built steadily, crescendoed, and died when Mr. Fenton cleared his throat.

"Mr. Murchinson, do you know the date of the Treaty of Paris?"

"Yes, sir. 1763."

"What did it signify?"

"The French turned over their empire in India and North America to the British. This angered the French middle class because it hurt them economically, and turned them against the king. It was the first seeds of the Revolution."

Mock applause broke out. Garrett told himself not to be flustered. He knew he was being tested in more ways than one.

"What was the first estate, Mr. Murchinson?"

"The first estate, or class, was the clergy."

"The second?"

"Nobility."

"Third?"

"The middle and lower classes, sir."

"Tell me about the fourth."

Garrett hesitated. "There was no such thing."

Mr. Fenton seemed impressed. "Let's try some more. I guess they teach history in Arkansas. When was the Bastille stormed? Year, month, day, and hour."

"July 14, 1789." He had no idea of the hour.

"Who was killed?"

"The governor of the prison and most of the guards."

"What was the long-term effect on the nobility?"

"Some fled. Others were guillotined. The rest agreed to reforms that gave vast power to the populace."

"Who was Marat?"

"The man responsible for the Reign of Terror."

"What was his personal affliction?"

"A skin disease."

"How was it treated?"

"With warm baths."

"Tell me his fate."

"Assassination."

"By whom?"

The questions flew at Garrett, but history was his favorite subject and he'd studied this time period and enjoyed it. When silence finally descended he felt an elation, even if no one acknowledged his victory. Mr. Fenton steered the discussion to the American Revolution. Other students volunteered answers now—Garrett could see there were some bright kids after all—but a few sneaked peeks into their notebooks. Garrett was surprised that Mr. Fenton didn't notice.

"Say, well done, Wyatt Earp." A thin boy with frizzy red hair came up afterward as they left the room. Garrett waited for him to pass, but he started mimicking Garrett's long, quick strides. Suddenly two more boys were in pursuit.

"Hey, cracker," one called. Garrett refused to turn. "Cracker, I'm talking to you."

Garrett kept moving. A thin, cold shaft of pain suddenly shot into his thigh. The pain turned hotter and blazed up his spine before he finally spun around. The red-haired boy met Garrett's fierce stare, and a low laugh sprung from his throat. He held up a shiny sewing needle.

Garrett already had his fist balled. The thought that he had not been in a fistfight for years didn't slow his reflex. His blow landed squarely in the boy's chest, fluttering him backward like a piece of paper.

"Hey, I'm impressed." The one who spoke had a crewcut and a hook nose and brown eyes set wide apart. He caught the red-haired boy before he fell. "Are you going to do that to me, too?" he asked.

"Yeah, hit us both, would you?" The third boy's hair swept back to his collar. He had stubble on his chin and thick, pouty lips.

"My name's Cleeb," Crewcut said, circling an arm around his friend. "This is Adam." The red-haired boy went unintroduced, as if he no longer mattered, or he'd had enough, and vanished into the small crowd of spectators.

"You're short, but you look pretty strong. You going to try out for the football team?" Adam quizzed Garrett.

"Maybe," he answered cautiously.

"That's wonderful, really," Cleeb gushed. "Adam and I are already on the team. Welcome." He extended a hand, but Garrett decided not to shake it. Cleeb wore a lopsided grin that dripped with sarcasm. Garrett walked on.

"Well, you have a nice day, too!" Cleeb shouted after him.

He could barely breathe. Blood and mucus clogged the back of his throat. All he could think about was a drink of water. His first day of school had been rough enough, and now his whole body was on fire. He was the shortest boy in the scrimmage huddle, but he asked for the ball again. Garrett hunkered behind the quarterback, his shoulder pads like boulders weighing him down.

From the sidelines he could feel the coach's eyes burning into him. The quarterback's count got lost in Garrett's raspy breathing. When he looked up, the ball was already floating toward him. He surged ahead, caught the pitch out in time, but didn't see Cleeb and Adam as he swept the corner. They came from behind, as he should have known they would. All practice they'd been blindsiding him, and each time the tackle was harder than the last. One seized his ankles now, while the other rammed his helmet into Garrett's chest. The ball squirted from his arms as he thudded to the ground.

"Hey, little man, you got to move faster," said Adam, hovering over the supine figure. He extended a hand, but Garrett didn't take it. "Want to try it again, little man?"

"Up yours," Garrett whispered. He picked himself up and shuffled back to the huddle. How much longer would his legs hold? He took in Cleeb's menacing stare. Garrett froze him right back. *Until you carry me out on a stretcher, I will keep letting you hit me. I won't let you intimidate me. I won't quit. I'm going to make this team. Nothing stops me when I want something. . . .*

On the next play, the quarterback tossed a quick flair pass. Garrett caught it in his belly and pivoted sharply, knowing Cleeb and Adam would be down his throat. But they were nowhere. Caught by surprise, Garrett lost his footing and slid backward in the grass. The laughter buried him like an avalanche. Pushing himself up, he didn't have the courage to look anyone in the eye. The coach's whistle split the air.

"I need another chance," Garrett said, head bowed, when Coach Enderbee sauntered over. Underneath his embarrassment Garrett felt anger, even if he didn't know with whom. He watched the rest of the team trot toward the gymnasium.

"I never cut anyone from the team until I've watched him a full week." Enderbee had a calmness that was reassuring.

"There were a lot of things I had to get used to today." Garrett kept excusing himself. "I felt I had a lot to prove—"

"I've still got my eyesight, son. I know what they were doing to you. I hope I see you tomorrow."

"You will," Garrett promised, feeling better. But in the gym, ignored by almost everyone, he felt himself lose his confidence. Showered and dressed, he plodded to the bus stop, suddenly angry again, and now he knew with whom. *He* was to blame. In Rainbow he had fit in because the town was so small, the boundaries were clear. Just because he'd moved to Los Angeles, he couldn't expect the city to adjust to *him*. Maybe he hadn't started the battle with Cleeb and Adam, but he would be the one to end it by not giving them any excuse to make him a target. He wanted to be accepted at his new school, and make the football team. He noticed a clothing store across from the bus stop. Garrett had just cashed a large check from Monroe. He didn't think about it twice.

Boarding the bus half an hour later was a juggling act.

First his books slipped from his arms, and then the packages. He tried not to think of his buying spree as extravagant. It was a necessity. When he reached home the aroma of dinner wafted from the kitchen, but Clarence wasn't around.

He removed his old clothes and stuffed everything in his suitcases—then pushed the bags to the back of the closet for good. In minutes the hangers were transformed by new jeans, two blazers, new shirts.

"Garrett—"

"Jeez, you scared me," he said when he turned and took in his father. When he looked again his chin trembled with laughter. "What is this—"

"Do you like it?"

It was Clarence who grinned now, as Garrett circled him warily. The old football from the living room was in the crook of his father's elbow. Faded and ripped in back, the burgundy jersey from his Chicago high school days stretched tightly over the shoulders and rode above his belt line. A gold 21 had lost its luster, but Garrett could easily see his father fading back to pass, sidestepping a tackle.

"Guts and glory!" Garrett exulted.

"Thirteen in a row!" Clarence roared. He made a mock pass, zinging the ball into Garrett's belly. His father led him to the front yard, where he attached a rope and old tire to the apple tree. Walking off fifteen paces, Clarence cocked his arm.

"I think you need an oil can," Garrett said with a poker face when the ball sailed five feet wide.

"Unbelievable!" Clarence's second toss was even wider of the mark.

Garrett chuckled as he retrieved each ball, but he saw the determination and focus in his father. Finally one ball spiraled through the tire, then another, and another. When it was Garrett's turn he was suddenly nervous. He felt he had to prove something, just like at school today.

"Bull's-eye!" his father exclaimed as the pass whizzed through the hole.

Garrett threw five winners in a row. Pleased, he felt his confidence grow. He could stay all night and never miss.

"You're in the zone, son. Why weren't you a quarterback like me?"

Too small, Garrett thought, or maybe he just never had anyone beside his mother to give him the encouragement. Monroe had always thought football was too dangerous.

"Here—move back to the fence," Clarence exhorted. Garrett walked off another fifteen paces. He clucked his tongue, then rifled the ball through the tire.

"Bravo!" Clarence shot his arms in the air.

They spurred one another on for an hour, laughing whenever they missed, which wasn't often, until Garrett's miserable day on the practice field seemed like a million years ago.

When the air began to cool he ambled back to his room. He remembered what his mother had said about his father's being a perfectionist, hard to live with. The perfection part seemed true—look at how Clarence had kept throwing the football until he succeeded—but Garrett had seen a fun side to his father, too. Why didn't his mother pay more attention to that? Maybe if she had, they would have gotten along better. Maybe his father would never have left. Maybe there'd never have been a car accident. . . .

Suddenly he could see all three standing together, Garrett half a head taller than his mother now, his father smiling, arms linked around each other. The image was so sharp and perfect. It seemed as real as a photograph. His eyes cut to his bedside table and took in his mother's pretty, slender face, the dimple in each cheek, as if at any moment she would step out of the frame and come back to life. Garrett tried to fight the hollow feeling. He'd never have his mother near him again. At least now he'd have a chance to have a father.

5

Progress. Garrett measured it in inches, but at least he was moving forward. On the bus home from football practice, he sat in the back row, away from passengers, to focus on homework. His schedule was finely tuned. He followed dinner with three to four hours of studying, and was in bed by ten so he could wake at six. He had been at Wilshire Academy not quite three weeks, but academically he was near the top in all his classes. He had survived the cut for the football team. Maybe he wouldn't be a starter, but he would see playing time. All he lacked at his new school were real friends and more than superficial respect. That would come. His new clothes were a help; so was his attitude. He had apologized to Tom, the boy with frizzy red hair, even though Garrett didn't care for him, and to Adam and Cleeb, whom he did like after all.

The bus stop was six short blocks from Garrett's house. He knew Clarence would already be in the kitchen. His father, a gourmet cook, was continually coming up with surprises. Whenever he traveled abroad, Clarence said, he tried to bring back one new recipe. Garrett wondered if, along with the piano, he shouldn't try to learn cooking, too—if only he had the time.

When he opened the front door he smelled something sweet and pungent, but it wasn't food. Even when he focused on the stranger in the living room, Garrett couldn't place the smell until the man rose and Garrett spotted the pipe in his hand. His father strolled from the kitchen wearing a red-and-white checkerboard apron.

"Garrett," Clarence said warmly, "this is my dearest and oldest friend, Quentin Abbey. Don't worry about making conversation with Quentin—he talks almost as much as I do. I should know. Our desks sit next to each other at the plant."

His father returned to making dinner as Garrett's puzzled glance settled on the guest. Clarence never talked about close friends. Quentin looked in his mid-fifties, older than Garrett's father. His hair was thinning front and back, and the jowly face had puffy bags around the eyes. His pipe and rumpled suit made him seem comfortable with himself. There was something immediately likable about him. While Garrett thought of his father as having finely polished edges, Quentin was all soft pockets and folds, like a teddy bear.

"So you're enrolled at Wilshire Academy," Quentin offered as he sat and relit his pipe. "Are you liking it?"

"I'm starting to. There's a lot of homework, more than at my last school."

"What about friends?"

"I'm starting to make some."

"What *don't* you like about Wilshire?"

Garrett had to think. "Kids cheat and are really competitive," he said frankly. "The school has an honor code, but no one seems to turn anyone in or get caught, either. What amazes me is that for such a brainy school the cheaters are even sloppy, but the system is worse. Everyone is grade-conscious. Everyone is after an A. I have to work hard, but I won't cheat." He thought for a second. "If I had to outsmart the system, I'd be a lot more clever."

"And being so smart, what college have you set your sights on?"

"It's almost time to apply. I'm still not sure, but maybe Columbia."

"Like your father!"

Garrett nodded. "Did you go to Columbia, too?"

"Yale," he said.

"Then when did you meet my father?"

Quentin's lips pursed into a reminiscing smile. "In 1979 I was in Helsinki, Finland, speaking at an international symposium. Concerned Scientists for World Peace. Clarence attended my seminar. We've been fast friends ever since, and worked at the same company now for two."

"I haven't met very many scientists," Garrett admitted, feeling a little out of his depth. His part of Arkansas was a cultural backwater. There were so many things he'd missed out on, but in Los Angeles he would turn all that around. "What kind of scientist are you?"

"My degree from Yale was in metallurgy, but my specialization is engineering, or industrial, photography." Quentin saw Garrett's quizzical look and continued with a smile. "Let me explain the field this way. Using sophisticated cameras, my colleagues and I can monitor movement phases of machinery, like relays and switches, or spot fractures in metals and plastics, or insulation breakdown. When our company builds a jet fighter, for example, it's essential to know how much stress and fatigue the plane will endure at high altitudes. A camera can tell us all that."

"Like in a jet engine?" Garrett said, recalling the soundproof lab where his father said he worked.

"Exactly."

"But how can a camera do that?" Garrett was fascinated. His idea of a camera was the old thirty-five-millimeter his mother had had.

"The process is known as high-speed photography, Garrett. A very special camera and technology can show the rapid succession of very small events—like the arc of a spark plug, or the detonation waves of dynamite—that occur much too fast for the naked eye to comprehend. Or take the field of biomechanics. With a high-jumper or pole-vaulter, for example, a high-speed camera can capture every split second that his body is in motion, record every critical movement. That's an invaluable tool. The athlete can study the photographs to see what he's doing wrong."

"Maybe I could use that on the football field," Garrett joked. "This is all new stuff, isn't it?"

"Not really. In the late 1800s a photographer named Mybridge settled an ancient argument about whether a race horse ever has all four hooves in the air at the same time. Mybridge had a very primitive camera by today's standards, but for its time the shutter speed was advanced. Through a series of exposures taken about every one-hundredth of a second, he proved that all four hooves *were* in the air at once. Ironically, one type of high-speed camera, a variation of the streak, or smear, camera—it's called synchronballistic—is used today at racetracks to record photo finishes."

"But how can a shutter work that fast?"

"It's quite complex. Basically, there're two kinds of high-speed cameras, the mechanical and the electro-optical. Each commonly allows for exposures of less than one-millionth of a second, which is called a microsecond. By comparison, a conventional mechanical shutter, as in a thirty-five-millimeter camera, allows for an exposure of only one four-thousandth of a second."

"You mean," Garrett said, making the equation in his head, "that a camera can shoot a million frames per second?"

"Actually," Quentin replied, "a state-of-the-art electro-optical camera can yield *ten* million frames. It's impossible for the imagination to conceive of something moving so fast—there're no comparisons in nature—but technology is unlimited."

"I don't understand," Garrett said. "If the camera takes ten million frames a second, or even a million, how can you process all that film? I mean, ten million. . . ."

Quentin smiled patiently. "There are different kinds of high-speed cameras, but if you take the electro-optical, or electronic, only five to ten images are ever printed on a piece of film. They're captured, of course, in a fraction of a microsecond. The trick is to set the shutter off at the right moment, so that the five or ten images received in sequence are the ones you want. You're never dealing with a million or ten million frames, only a handful."

Garrett's mind raced with a hundred questions as he listened to Quentin, but he settled on just one. "How involved is my father in all this?"

"Clarence and I share virtually all our work and research. We're a team."

As talkative as his father was, he revealed almost nothing about his highly sensitive job. Garrett was determined to learn more about his father, and Quentin was a great source.

"Shall we go?" Clarence had his apron off.

"Go where?" Garrett asked.

"If you'd excuse us, Garrett," Clarence said, "Quentin and I have a meeting to attend. We won't be gone long. Afterward we can all enjoy a leisurely meal."

"Sure," Garrett said accommodatingly, but he wondered why he couldn't join them. "What kind of meeting?" he asked.

A smile crinkled Clarence's rugged face. "You have homework, I believe."

"I'm ahead on my assignments. If it's only an hour or so, it won't be a problem."

"You might not be interested."

"Why not let him come?" Quentin interrupted.

His father finally relented. A few miles beyond the freeway was a small church. A couple dozen people already filled the pews as Garrett sat quietly next to his father. Quentin marched toward the pulpit, his hands clasped in front of him. He smiled warmly at the crowd.

"Good evening, I'm Quentin Abbey," he began. "I want to thank everyone for coming tonight. We have petitions for you to sign, but first I want to say a few words about tonight's short movie.

"We're all aware of the recent winds of global political change. *Glasnost* in the Soviet Union, the mass exodus of fed-up citizens from Eastern bloc countries, and the changes that have toppled the cruelest communist governments. The cry worldwide for human rights is overwhelming . . . yet our own government seems as blind and distrusting as ever. Opportunities for world peace have never been clearer or more genuine. Why do our leaders treat them as excuses for isolationism, or only pay lip service to decreasing our defense budget?"

Applause kept interrupting Quentin. His voice was warm and caring. It filled the church like a hymn before the room finally went dark. Almost from the start the movie terrified Garrett. How could his father think he might not have been interested? His throat went dry, his limbs tingled. Could this really happen? The fictional drama of a nuclear attack on the United States was unfathomable in its consequences, yet the movie scenes were so real. Buildings vaporized in seconds. People afflicted with radiation died slow and agonizing deaths. Garrett had chills long after the lights went back on.

"That was a nightmare," he whispered as the three left the church and drove home. Garrett felt almost guilty. World politics seemed so much more relevant than his narrow concerns of finding himself in his new home and school. It was obvious that his father and Quentin cared deeply. The irony that they worked for a defense contractor yet were both seriously involved in a world peace movement was almost comforting. They were an inspiration. They were strong individuals. They had a right, maybe a duty, to let their consciences speak. When Garrett thought about it, he didn't see how anyone, no matter what his profession, could ignore the cause of world peace.

"Did you learn something tonight?" Clarence asked Garrett. "Most people see a movie like that, and they pretend it's an unpleasant fantasy. The truth is it could

37

really happen. It will happen, unless we achieve a true balance of world power."

"How long have you been involved in groups like this?"

"Off and on since I returned from Vietnam."

"Your father," Quentin broke in, "is usually the one to speak at these meetings. He has a way of commanding attention. People listen to him. You should be very proud of him."

At home it was hard deciding which Garrett enjoyed more, his father's lamb curry and stir-fried vegetables, or the charged conversation. Like a philosopher-king, Clarence expounded with authority on many subjects. Garrett kept thinking how lucky he was to be living with his father and being exposed to new ideas.

When the phone rang Clarence answered in the kitchen. He looked pleased when he returned to the table.

"Quentin, old friend, that was supervisor Kealy. Time to pack our bags."

Garrett flicked his head between the two friends. "Where are you going?"

"Quentin and I are off to Seoul again."

"South Korea?" Garrett felt a stirring of envy. He had always wanted to travel to the Orient. "For how long?"

"Just a week," Clarence said. "We're consulting with a Korean aerospace firm on a joint project."

"I didn't know the South Koreans were that advanced technologically," Garrett said. "Are they like the Japanese?"

"They're getting closer, and they're light-years ahead of North Korea."

Garrett knew something about the Korean War and General MacArthur, and that the two countries—North and South—were still bitter enemies. The communist North, while recently opening its doors to Western visitors, was still mostly a closed and secretive society.

"Garrett, I can have a neighbor look in on you—"

"You don't have to. I'll be fine."

"You're sure?"

"Absolutely." Didn't his father see yet? He could be just as independent and responsible as an adult.

"I'll leave you money for groceries and any emergencies. And for gas. Take the car to school whenever you like."

"The bus is fine. But thanks." He was grateful for the trust, but he felt he couldn't park Clarence's old wreck in the Wilshire Academy lot. He'd be laughed off campus.

Garrett cleared the dishes and padded toward his room when he noticed his father reaching for something in the hallway closet. A sturdy vinyl case came down. Garrett watched as his father gently pulled out what looked like a camcorder—a home video camera—but this model was all white, very sleek, with more buttons and controls. Space age, he thought, intrigued. Garrett caught his distorted reflection in the long, narrow lens.

"What is it?"

"One of those high-speed electronic cameras we spoke about," Quentin explained as he walked up.

"You're taking it to Korea?"

"Most every trip," his father affirmed.

Garrett wanted to touch the camera, but Clarence was holding it too possessively. In the closet he spotted several other cases.

"More cameras," his father said, watching Garrett's eyes. "Mechanical. Streak. All very exotic and extremely expensive. They're not toys."

"No," Garrett agreed, but he wanted to play with them anyway.

In his room, he labored through algebra and English while his father and Quentin talked in the living room about science and engineering. Garrett kept listening. He wanted to sit in. After history, science was his favorite subject.

Quentin didn't leave until almost eleven. Garrett saw that his father already had his suitcase packed and by the door. Settled on the couch with a book, Clarence looked up with his clear eyes. He never seemed to need much sleep.

"Will I see you in the morning?" Garrett asked.

"Not unless you're up by five. Don't worry. Get your rest. School's what's important. I'll be back before you know it."

"Have a great trip. Good night, Dad." Garrett walked over and gave him a hug. It was the first time he had done that, he realized, or called Clarence "Dad."

In bed he waited in the grainy darkness, but he was too exhausted to sleep. His legs still ached from football practice, and algebra equations flashed through his head. He stirred when he heard his father's voice. Had Quentin come back? No, he realized, Clarence was on the phone. Garrett's head rose from the pillow as he strained to hear. But his father kept his voice deliberately low, a hoarse whisper, like there was something secret going on, Garrett thought in frustration, and finally he closed his ears.

6

"**F**our, twenty-six, nineteen, zero-zero—"

The ball zipped from the quarterback's sure hands to Garrett's. *Catch me now*, he thought as he broke two waist tackles and surged toward a sliver of light. Adam and Cleeb pursued with a vengeance. Garrett cut to avoid a linebacker, giving his old enemies a chance to catch him, but when they were within a hair's breadth he accelerated. As he crossed the goal, he saw Enderbee scribbling furiously on his clipboard. The coach didn't look overjoyed about his defensive coverage, but he had to be impressed with his halfback.

"Nice run," Cleeb allowed as the team trotted to the showers.

"Thanks." Garrett shook Cleeb's hand. Adam was right behind, his purple face struggling for air. Maybe it was a small miracle, but Garrett had always believed his hard work would pay dividends. Too bad his father was still in Korea, and not here to see how Garrett was improving. He and Adam and Cleeb were on good terms, too. Sometimes the three had lunch together, and over the weekend they'd taken in a movie.

"You guys up for anything tonight?" Garrett asked as the three stepped into the showers. He had gotten so far ahead on his homework, he only had a history paper to start.

"School night." Adam declined as the steam swirled around them.

"What have you got in mind?" Cleeb flashed his trademark grin.

"There's a Mozart festival at the Hollywood Bowl."

"Mozart?" Water spit off Adam's pouty lips. "What is this, high culture? Or are you bucking for a spot on the Wilshire faculty?"

Cleeb's rubbery face stayed lit with mischief. The chocolate brown eyes positively beamed. "Look, if you want to do something a little different, Adam and I can be your guides." His head swung to his sidekick. "Your folks won't kill you if you get home a little late tonight, will they?"

Adam shrugged. "Okay, count me in."

Garrett thought for only a second. Culture was nice— Mozart was something he could tell his dad about—but if he really wanted to explore the city. . . . "Where do I meet you guys?"

It was dusk when he drove his father's car to an address off Hollywood Boulevard. A breeze sweetened the air as he rolled down his window and checked the address again. Cleeb's new BMW was parked in front. Garrett couldn't help feeling a little resentful. There was so much wealth at his school, mirroring the pockets of Los Angeles that Clarence had driven him through, that Garrett couldn't pretend it didn't affect him.

Embarrassed, Garrett parked his father's clunker a block away and traipsed back to the bar and lounge. In the shadowy spaces, his eyes paraded over the mostly empty stools before he spotted Adam and Cleeb in a booth, and he marched over.

"What are you guys doing in this dump?" Garrett was reluctant even to sit. This was Cleeb's idea of a special evening?

"Drinking the coldest beer in Los Angeles." Adam beckoned to the disheveled woman behind the bar. She was the size of a bank vault door.

"That's Large Marge," Cleeb whispered to Garrett. "Proprietress extraordinaire. She never cards us. Hey, you do drink, don't you?"

"Sure," Garrett said self-consciously. Reluctantly he settled in the booth.

"Cheers," Cleeb toasted when they all had fresh glasses. "To the Masters of the Universe!"

Garrett's head twisted up. "Masters of what?"

Cleeb didn't respond. They finished their beers, trading patter, until Garrett asked again.

"Masters of the Universe," Cleeb repeated. "Wanna play?"

"Play what? What are you talking about?"

"You never saw the toy, or the video game?" Adam asked, astonished. "What did you do in that pissant little Arkansas town?"

"I was pretty busy with school, and helping my mother," he said honestly.

"What about free time?"

"I didn't have much."

"But when you did?"

"Taking apart and fixing up old cars, mostly." Garrett felt pathetic again—he was so out of it—like he'd lived his whole life in a cave. "Look," he said, "I came to L.A. to get away from all that. I want to be exposed to new things."

Cleeb ordered another round. "Then this is tailor-fit for you, Murchinson."

"What is?"

"To become a Master of the Universe," Adam spoke. "What else?"

"A Master of the Universe is afraid of nothing," Cleeb explained. "He has unlimited imagination, absolute power, uncanny strength, and endless energy. He does anything he wants. He accepts all challenges, all risks, and is

43

afraid of nothing, absolutely nothing, including failure—
because that's where his power comes from."

Garrett's brow folded in confusion.

"Don't you see?" Cleeb asked. "When you know there's
nothing that can stop you, you can do anything."

"Absolute power," Adam verified. "And the beauty is
that no one knows it but you. A Master of the Universe
never tells. He doesn't need to. He's totally self-contained,
and the secrecy gives him even greater powers."

Cleeb nodded. "Adam and I have never told another
soul about our own version of the game—you're the first.
Are you in?"

Garrett swallowed a laugh. "You guys are setting me up—"

"No way," Cleeb swore. "This is our private little
club."

Garrett began to see his friends were serious. "Okay.
Why me?"

"Because you're different from most kids. You showed
some character the first day of school—standing up to us
when we harassed you. Then a couple of days later you
made friends with us. That showed even more character."

"Can I tell my father about this?"

"Absolutely nobody."

Garrett lolled his head back. "Is this dangerous?"

"That depends on your definition," Adam said thoughtfully. "What we do is never physically dangerous, but
sometimes we break laws. There has to be a challenge.
Something to test a Master of the Universe."

Garrett worked on his second beer. Cleeb's and Adam's
tone had become more convincing. He had to admit he
was intrigued. This would never have happened in Rainbow.
No one there was that creative or bold.

"I'm in," he heard his voice say.

"Great!" Cleeb exulted. "We'll start off small. Your
maiden voyage won't be arduous. You'll just get your toes
wet. You'll feel the first ripples of power. See the movie
theater across the street?"

Garrett turned. The theater was modest and slightly

44

run-down, like the neighborhood. "ACK TO THE FUTURE 2" was emblazoned across the marquee.

"Three weeks ago I took down the *B*. I won't tell you how, just that I didn't get caught. Tonight you're going to remove the *A*. We'll be right here. You've got thirty minutes."

Garrett started to laugh. It was just a prank.

"Take it seriously," Cleeb warned, "and you'll see the rewards. Let yourself be challenged. This is a question of attitude. Tell yourself you'll never be caught . . . that's what's crucial. That's where the power comes in."

Garrett's fingers tingled as he marched across the street. Perhaps his two beers gave him false courage, but he had never felt more alive. He stood under the marquee and appraised the distance to the letters. The teenage girl in the ticket booth was filing her nails. The sidewalk was fairly empty. An all-night drugstore suddenly caught his eye. His adrenaline opened the doors of his imagination, gave him a rush of confidence. He could have no doubts of his success. Weren't those the rules of the game?

In his most convincing voice, he asked the drugstore manager if he could borrow a ladder. There was an emergency down the street—a cat was stuck in a tree. The lie bothered Garrett a little as he took the ladder, but he quickly forgave himself. What did an insignificant lie matter if the ultimate purpose was far more important? At the theater he rested the top rungs against the marquee and clambered up brazenly, as if he worked at the theater. He grabbed his prize and returned the ladder. He was sure the girl in the booth hadn't even noticed him.

"Nine minutes on the button," Cleeb declared with a peek at his watch and admiration in his voice. "It took me fifteen. I climbed a fire escape to the roof, and reached the marquee with a coat hanger. Your way was a lot gutsier. I'm impressed."

"Did you ever doubt your success?" Adam asked Garrett.

"No," Garrett said honestly, thinking about it. He'd had no doubts at all. That's what had been so much fun.

45

"Welcome to the club," Adam said, and ordered everyone another round.

Garrett was home by nine to start his history paper. The stunt was still fresh in his mind; so was his sense of satisfaction. Maybe Adam and Cleeb were right. He felt a new energy, a new power. He thought he could accomplish anything. His history assignment, to analyze economic class struggles since the Middle Ages, was going to get an A; there was no doubt. He had read for a week on the vast subject and knew what he wanted to say. He was going to pull A's in all his classes because he expected nothing less for himself. Time permitting, he'd start filling out college applications tonight, including the one for Columbia.

It was after midnight when his eyes began to close. In the kitchen he poured himself some orange juice and gazed into the empty living room. He missed his father, but he also enjoyed having the house to himself. Friends were nice, even necessary—tonight had been great fun— but he didn't mind being alone and having his own space, too. He had always liked the feeling of self-reliance.

On his way to the bedroom he stopped at the hallway closet. *No,* he thought, *you're tired, go to bed.* He turned the knob anyway. Clarence hadn't explicitly forbidden him to look at the cameras, had he? Garrett would be careful. Nothing would be damaged. How could he hope to know more about his father if he didn't understand his work? How could he expand his own small world unless he investigated things he didn't know? If he was a true Master of the Universe. . . .

He took down the three heavy cases from the top shelf, careful not to trip over the tripod leaning in a corner. The first case clicked open just as the phone shrilled. Garrett froze, as if caught in some guilty act. Who would be calling at midnight? Wrong number, had to be. Or was it his father from Korea?

"Hello?" he breathed, after sprinting to the phone.

Static hummed in his ear.

46

"Hello? Dad?" The interference crackled again, as if the caller were a million miles away. Garrett felt someone was on the line, but all he heard was a series of weird clicks. "Dad? Hello? Is that you?"

He hung up in disappointment and returned to exploring. The first camera looked vastly different from the one Quentin and his father had taken to Korea. A streak, or smear camera, he guessed, the type similar to the one Quentin said was used for photo finishes. Two distinct parts fit on a single track—a long, narrow lens, and what looked like the camera proper. The two were separated by a space of several inches. Garrett saw that the lens could be moved closer or farther from the camera, which probably increased or decreased lens magnification. Quentin had said that the principle behind the camera was that once received by the lens, a blur or smear of light, calculated against the time taken to record an event like the arc of a spark plug, revealed the distance the object had traveled.

A button released the back latch, and Garrett glimpsed circuit boards, wires, and a long, narrow tube that reminded him of a sealed vacuum tube in a TV. How did it all work? He knew the answer was probably complex, but that only whetted his interest. He found a magnifying glass in his father's desk and started to look closer when the phone shrilled again.

"Hello?" he said.

The same static hum filled his ear.

"Hello! Can anyone hear me? Hello! Hello!"

He realized he was shouting. The phone was suddenly no longer a phone but some inanimate object that made him look stupid. He only paid half attention to the crackling sound as he hung up impatiently and went back to his cameras.

7

The next day after football Garrett took the bus as far as the public library. In the card catalog he could find only one book on industrial photography. Gathering dust, it looked as if it had never been opened. In a quiet room he cradled his chin in his hands. The shutter on the mechanical camera that Quentin had spoken of was called a Faraday shutter, he read. It consisted of a glass cylinder placed inside a magnetic coil between two crossed polarizing filters. So long as the two filters remain crossed, no light could pass through. But whenever a current pulsed through the coil to generate a magnetic field, the polarization in the cylinder was affected, and light permeated the second filter, just long enough—a microsecond—to expose an image on film. The electro-optical shutter, or Kerr cell, was made up of a liquid cell of nitrobenzene fitted with electrodes and, similar to the Faraday shutter, was placed between two crossed polarizers. An electric pulse applied to the electrodes changed the polarization properties of the nitrobenzene so that light was briefly transmitted. An image converter tube in the camera transmitted the optical image focused on one end of the tube onto a phosphorescent screen at the other end.

Garrett read the page a half dozen times before he tackled the section on electronic flashes. For high-speed cameras, sparks were discharged between electrodes in quick bursts called nanoseconds. Sometimes miniature lasers with switching modes were employed that could cut flash durations to a fraction of a nanosecond. Multiple flash impulses were designed to go off in rapid succession, and could photograph either a stationary or a moving subject with phenomenal accuracy and clarity.

Garrett reached home well after dark in a warm drizzle. He took off his wet clothes and tidied up the house. His father was due back tomorrow, but part of Garrett wished he'd stay away longer. He wanted more time with the cameras. Putting his history paper on hold, he spent hours examining the three models again, trying to apply what he'd learned in the library. He was pleased he was able to grasp some of the principles. He knew it took a special knack to understand, a knowledge of mechanics. He'd gotten some of that from taking apart old cars.

The phone rang. Garrett turned with annoyance. It was almost the same time last night that he'd gotten the strange calls. Was this a prank? He suddenly wondered if Adam and Cleeb were behind this. Picking up the receiver, Garrett just held it to his ear.

"Hello?" sang a nasal voice. "Who's there? Garrett? Garrett Woolsey?"

His chest deflated. "Monroe!" His uncle's soft drawl made him laugh, and conscious of his own speech. "Monroe, it's the middle of the night—what's going on? Hey, did you try to call me last night?"

"What? No. I couldn't sleep tonight. And you haven't called me in so long, I was getting worried. Did I wake up your father? Is there a problem?"

49

"No, Monroe. I'm fine. So's Dad." Garrett had gotten so busy, he'd forgotten not just Monroe but his entire life and his old friends from Rainbow. He didn't call it home anymore. He wondered if he was doing it subconsciously, just to put his mom's death behind him. Now he was glad Monroe had called. He still felt close to his uncle, even though Garrett was glad to be part of a new life.

"What's it like in L.A., Garrett?"

"It's different. You wouldn't believe it, Monroe. The city's one big fast lane. At first I wasn't too sure about my school, but now I like it a lot. And I made the football team."

"I knew you'd succeed, Garrett! You can do anything you set your mind to. Now tell me—Clarence, how's he?"

"Traveling right now. He's a real nice guy, real understanding. Mother was right when she told me he was different. He's an idealist with strong opinions, sort of a philosopher. We get along beautifully. He trusts me, he respects my judgment. I don't see how it could be any easier."

"Too bad—I thought I could talk you into coming home!"

They both laughed. Garrett knew there was no way he'd go back to Rainbow now. He was in L.A. for good. He promised Monroe he'd be the one to call next. When he'd hung up, he returned the cameras to the closet and made certain that nothing was out of place. He looked around to be sure everything looked the same. Suddenly an envelope he'd never noticed peeked out from a corner. He couldn't resist opening the flap.

Inside he found a single photo, black-and-white and slightly blurry. In the foreground, a series of straight, thin, symmetrical lines didn't seem to be anything Garrett could make out. In the distance he spied what looked like a postage stamp. He picked up the magnifying glass that he'd carefully put away, but what he was able to see hardly helped. There was a grainy pattern to the stamp, some kind of design, but it was so faint that he couldn't tell what.

He knew it would give away that he'd been snooping around the cameras if he asked his father what the photo meant. He put everything back in place and drifted to his room, much too full of curiosity to sleep right away.

8

"Four days to the season opener—" Cleeb winked at Large Marge and raised his glass. "To victory!"

"Dominate and devastate!" Adam thundered from their booth.

"Annihilate and decapitate!" Garrett ended the Wilshire fight song with a wry smile. At the moment he didn't think he could inflict damage on a gnat. Every bone and muscle ached from practice. Right now all he wanted was to recuperate. His second day in a row in this dumpy bar actually made him feel better. It was a good place to get away, to hide, when you needed it.

"Cleeb and I are giving a party after the game." Adam's words broke into his thoughts. "My folks are away. You're coming, aren't you?"

"Sure," Garrett said. "Do I need a date?"

Cleeb ran his hand over his crewcut. "Yours truly has already invited the young lovelies from our sister school, Winchester. Just bring yourself, Murchinson."

Adam ordered more beers and was ready to discuss the next adventure for the Masters of the Universe, but Garrett begged off. "It's almost seven," he said, moving stiffly as he rose. "I've got tons of algebra." He patted the book under his arm. "The life of a slave."

"Work hard, party hard," Adam summarized.

"See you guys tomorrow."

"Not unless we see you first."

"Yeah, yeah. . . ." Garrett took a mock swing at Adam before waving good night. He was starting to really like his new friends. These two were different from all the guys he'd known back home. In a short period of time Garrett felt close to them. He hadn't really talked about his mother, but he felt that he probably could if he wanted to. These guys liked him—appreciated him for his guts. It made him feel good.

When he arrived home after dark he found Quentin's car in the drive. Surprised, he hustled up the walkway. In the living room his father's large frame hovered over an open trunk that brimmed with colorful packages. Clarence spun around and gave Garrett a bear hug. He seemed incredibly fresh and full of energy, as if he'd traveled only across town instead of across the Pacific. Perched on the piano bench, a rumpled, disheveled Quentin offered Garrett a tired salute.

"I didn't think you'd get in till late," Garrett explained. "I would have had dinner for you."

"Don't worry. We ate our way through Korea," Quentin said, focusing on his ample belly.

"How was the trip?" Garrett asked excitedly.

"A resounding success, wouldn't you say, Quentin? All our testing and research went without a hitch. Garrett, for you," Clarence said with his usual rush of energy, picking several packages from the trunk. Garrett was embarrassed. What was this, Christmas? He hadn't gotten his father anything. All he'd wanted was Clarence home safely. Still, he liked opening the first present, a hugh ceramic bowl with a deep patina and intricate design. It had to have cost a mint. So did the antique lacquered painting and tasteful, hand-carved bird he unwrapped next.

"Now your room won't be so bare," Clarence said.

"Thanks, really—they're beautiful. How did you afford them, or carry this big chest around?" His father didn't answer. "What else did you buy?" Garrett asked as he peered into the trunk, which now seemed like a treasure chest.

"Small things. Personal things. An occasional company bonus comes in handy. I never said money was totally evil, did I? It's a means to an end. Education, objects of beauty or historical interest, travel, good food—to me these things are worth their price."

"I want to hear all about your trip," Garrett said.

His father, always willing to talk about general things, began to describe busy Seoul, where traffic was as formidable as in Los Angeles. He went on about how fanatical Koreans were concerning sports and recreation. He began a dissertation, or so it seemed to Garrett, about the South's ever-present fear and suspicion of the North. Quentin added a few stories of his own and finally said he'd head home for the night. Garrett felt a little sorry for his father's friend. He wasn't married and didn't have family in L.A. His work was his life, Clarence had once commented. Garrett didn't doubt that commitment, even contentment, but it was still a life that seemed isolated and lonely. Maybe that was how his father's life was before Garrett arrived. Maybe that was why Clarence had invited him to L.A., to have his son close to him and not be alone any longer.

"You manage okay while I was gone?" Clarence asked when he strolled into Garrett's room.

Garrett twisted around at his desk. He'd been waiting for his father to ask. "Everything was perfect. I almost never used the car. I've got money left over. I did some work in your garden. No problems at all." He felt proud for being so responsible.

"And your homework? You're on top of everything?" Clarence was suddenly peering through Garrett's papers from the week. "What's this?"

Garrett stared at the red C at the top of his English exam. It had been a surprise for him, too, just like the quiz sprung at the end of the period yesterday. Too busy with Cleeb and Adam, and playing with the cameras, he hadn't been prepared. "It's never happened before," Garrett excused himself. "Don't worry, because I'm not. I'm getting mostly A's. With football and everything, it's hard to keep up every second."

"What's everything?" Clarence asked, concerned. He half sat on Garrett's desk, looking down. "Didn't you study while I was gone?"

"Of course I studied." Garrett didn't understand why his father was suddenly nervous about his schoolwork. "A couple of nights I went out with friends—"

"Like tonight? Is that why you were late? I smell beer on your breath."

"I just had one or two. I would have told you."

"But on a school night," Clarence pointed out. "Is that being responsible?"

Garrett struggled for a defense. He hadn't expected this. He had expected to be complimented for keeping everything together on the home front. His father's tone was reasonable—he never raised his voice—yet the words stung.

"Garrett," Clarence said, rising from his perch and dropping on the bed, "I probably don't need to remind you—you're a very conscientious boy, and I'm proud of you—but don't you see the dangers around you? The temptations? I'm not telling you whom to choose as friends, but I urge you to think about your values."

"What about my values?" He had never really thought about the subject as a choice. He was hardworking, responsible—or he thought he was, until tonight. What was there to think about?

"There're some things I've noticed, that's all," Clarence said. "I wasn't going to say anything, but maybe I should. You won't think I'm coming down hard on you, will you?"

"Of course not," he said, meaning it.

"Well, first, all those new clothes you bought—"

"What about them?"

"What made you act so impulsively?"

He thought it was obvious. "Because I wanted to feel more comfortable at school. I wanted to fit in."

"Were you feeling ashamed of who you were? Being from a different part of the country, or not having money or a fancy car like most kids at Wilshire—"

"I was feeling self-conscious," Garrett admitted. He wondered about his true feelings. He wasn't exactly ashamed, but he still felt like an outsider sometimes, despite his efforts to blend in. Money was a major part of it. Cleeb and Adam had never seen the old Ford he drove, or visited the small rental house where he lived, or been told what his father did. Maybe they thought he was as rich as they. He felt bad now for trying to hide everything. Why should he feel so self-conscious? If he truly wasn't ashamed, why not just tell his friends his limited circumstances? He had felt close enough to them to want to tell them about his mother. What were his values, anyway?

"You're sure about your choice of friends?" Clarence asked again.

"Cleeb and Adam are good guys." Garrett had scarcely mentioned them to his father. What would Clarence think about the Masters of the Universe, or the stunt Garrett had pulled? *Maybe I'm not so responsible after all,* he thought.

"I just want you to live up to your potential." Clarence encouraged him. "I only want what's best for you. Don't be distracted by a crowd, especially one with false values. Know your own values. Don't be afraid to stand up to the majority. We live in a city of seven million rats who chase their tails and worship at the altar of power, money, and success. Don't be fooled, son. There's nothing wrong with having a little fun, but remember your priorities."

Garrett nodded solemnly. He had known his father had high standards, and high expectations for him. Garrett didn't like disappointing people he cared about. He had tried never to disappoint his mother, and now he saw he would have to deal with his father's concerns. He would spend less time with Cleeb and Adam, and more on schoolwork—but would that be enough to make *him* happy? With his mother's death it had felt like everything had been ripped away from him. His eyes focused on his father on the bed. Clarence looked so remote suddenly, so formidable. The silence was a bridge between them that Garrett didn't know how to cross. And it echoed another silence, deep inside himself.

"Dad," he began, measuring carefully what he would say. He had practiced this speech countless times, over half a lifetime, yet now his mouth went dry. Where was his courage? He forced out the words. "Why didn't you ever phone or visit me?"

"What?" Clarence didn't seem to understand.

"All those years after you left, why didn't you keep in touch? I know you were busy, you traveled, you changed jobs—and I appreciated all the presents you sent—but couldn't you have come home just once, or called?"

Clarence's luminous eyes glided over him. "You've been thinking about this a long time, haven't you?"

Garrett grabbed a breath. "I never admitted it to Mom, or to Monroe—I always kept it inside—I guess I keep a lot of things to myself—but yeah, it bothered me. One reason I came to Los Angeles was finally to ask you, face-to-face. Was it something to do with me? Is that why you never came back?" He thought his heart would explode.

Clarence studied him and calmly replied, "I have never run from responsibilities. I certainly wasn't running from you. I love you, Garrett. That's the first thing you should know. The second is that I am what I am. A nomad, intellectually and otherwise. A dreamer, if you will, but a conscientious one. I never stop searching for answers, and there are new questions almost every day. If you find it hard to know me, you're not the first. Your mother always thought I left because I was frustrated and unhappy

57

within myself. Perhaps she was right—at least in part. I swear it had nothing to do with her or you."

"Then what did it have to do with?" Garrett asked. "What makes you so restless? What are you looking for? Why are your standards so high?"

"Garrett, except for you, and your mother, and a few friends along the way, like Quentin, people have always let me down. That's why I don't feel very many loyalties. That's why I'm so restless. I don't trust the world. Maybe you can understand better if I tell you something about my father. He was not exactly the loyal type. A salesman, he worked for more companies than you have fingers and toes. He was almost never home. And when he was, he drank. Oh, was he a drinker. The man must have been weaned on bourbon. I was raised by my mother."

"What was she like?" Garrett asked, more curious by the moment. He had waited so long for these answers. His mother never mentioned his father's parents, his grandparents. He'd never known them. "Was she like Mom?"

"Just the opposite, I'm afraid. A party girl. We didn't get along at all. Oh, she said she loved me, but I know she found me too aloof and quiet, too judgmental. I didn't like the way she was always at the beauty parlor or playing bridge or going to movies with her girlfriends. The woman threw away her life, didn't know what it meant to try hard at anything. I swore to myself at a very young age I would never be like her, or marry anyone like her."

"Is she still alive?"

"No."

"It sounds like you're still upset, like you think she abandoned you."

"Emotionally, there was no question that she did. I remember very clearly, Garrett. When I was seven or eight, she would leave me alone in the house for the whole day sometimes. Maybe that had a silver lining, because all that free time gave me a chance to read.

Everything I could put my hands on—magazines, newspapers, the dictionary, encyclopedias, novels, histories. I learned to love ideas. Ideas, I realized, could never disappoint me. Ideas were something I could be loyal to. I began to see how hypocritical and insincere the world was. I wanted to save it, and if I couldn't, at least I would save myself. I set my own standards and goals. I promised myself I would never compromise. As I saw more and learned from my experiences, my ideology went from one end of the spectrum to the other, but it never lacked sincerity and conviction. All I'd like from you, Garrett, is to have the same sense of purpose. I detest frivolity. We only have one life, and it's a cardinal sin to waste it."

Garrett was almost breathless from listening. There was something spellbinding about his father. Clarence's leaving had nothing to do with him. It was being abandoned as a child that made his father restless and idealistic.

But hadn't he deserted Garrett in a way? Not intentionally, not for the same reasons, but maybe the results had been the same. Garrett had always set goals for himself, too. Maybe he was always trying to prove something to his absent father.

Suddenly Garrett felt a bond with Clarence he could never have anticipated. His father had just left him alone again, the week he went to Korea. Garrett had used the time the way his father had when he was a boy—to learn something new, something he could prove himself with. Garrett decided that he wanted more than anything to have his father's love.

"Dad, when you were gone," Garrett said, finding his courage, "I took advantage of something that maybe I shouldn't have. I spent a lot of time with your cameras. I did some reading at the library, too, but mostly it was playing with the cameras that took up my time. That's why I got that C."

He expected, and thought he could handle, any reprimand he was surely due. But his father only put an understanding hand on his shoulder, nodded his head slowly as if he already knew, and let Garrett go back to his homework.

9

"I propose"—Cleeb lowered his voice as the three lounged under a tree outside the administration building—"that the Masters of the Universe act in unison. And I have the perfect plan." His brow lifted conspiratorially as the noontime flow of students circulated around them.

"Something worthy, something creative, I hope," Adam said loftily.

"Of course." The dark chocolate brown eyes aimed at Garrett. "We're going to stop school."

Garrett started to laugh. "Come again?"

"You talk about acts of ultimate power. . . . What can top bringing to a halt this redoubtable institution of higher learning, at least for a day? And I don't mean some stupid prank like setting off the fire alarm."

Adam's face contorted gravely. "Then what?"

"Oh, ye of little imagination. By the power of the word . . . the power of rumor."

Garrett picked up the cue. "Like a rumor about an earthquake, that the buildings aren't safe?"

"I like your thinking, Murchinson, but dig deeper. Try this on: We start telling everyone about the plague."

"What plague?" Adam said, confused.

"What plague? You mean you haven't heard? The insidious airborne virus that maims and sometimes kills in minutes, the one that's so volatile that anyone getting close to the victim is infected immediately? It started last year in southern Russia, then broke out in China, and now it's spread to India—only the governments there are keeping it quiet, to avoid wholesale panic.

"We tell a few kids, and they'll laugh, of course," Cleeb continued, "but in the back of their minds a seed of doubt begins to grow, enough for them to repeat the story to others. Soon the whole campus knows, including the faculty. Then, bam! One day I suddenly keel over in history class, right in front of dear Mr. Fenton, and seconds later, so do you, Murchinson; then Adam. . . ."

Cleeb's face lit up like a Christmas tree. "I'm willing to bet we clear out not only the classroom, but the whole school! The administration will call an ambulance, the city health department, the Centers for Disease Control in Atlanta. . . . Maybe they'll even phone the White House!"

"Think of the challenge," Adam declared, picking up his friend's enthusiasm. "Anyone else would be scared out of his mind to try this. . . . Think of the rush of power from having this much control!"

Garrett felt both his friends' eyes focus on him, waiting to confirm Cleeb's genius. The idea *was* imaginative, and maybe it would be successful. Part of Garrett wanted to try it, but he kept hearing his father's voice of caution.

"I don't know," Garrett said, stalling. "Maybe we should think about this for a few days. If the stunt backfires, we could look like total jerks, not Masters of the Universe."

"What can go wrong if we truly believe in it?" Cleeb asked. "That's the whole point. Someone else attempting this *would* look like a moron, but not us."

"Give me a few days," Garrett said.

He found himself avoiding Cleeb and Adam the rest of the day, and he was grateful football practice was no more than an inspirational play review for tomorrow's game.

61

The bus ferried him home early. By dinnertime he'd finished Friday's assignments and waded back into his paper on class economic conflict. He enjoyed studying the forces of history, the ferment of ideas. Nineteenth-century England was particularly horrifying—how could the working class have let itself be so exploited?

After an hour he turned off his computer. He was starved. Where was his father? The man who lived by schedules was sometimes early but never late. Garrett traipsed into the living room and peered into the darkened yard. No one answered when he called Clarence at work. He settled back at his desk, but his thoughts were too scattered for homework.

"Dad?" he called when the front door squeaked open.

He found his father on the piano bench, absently striking a couple of keys. Clarence lifted a tired gaze to Garrett. The usual ebullient smile was missing. Garrett noticed a cheap vinyl briefcase at his father's side. "It's been a very long day," Clarence answered the unspoken question.

Garrett nodded sympathetically. "Do you want some dinner?"

"Nothing for me, thanks. How about if I fix you something?"

Clarence didn't talk as he puttered in the kitchen. *This time the uncomfortable silence has nothing to do with me,* Garrett thought. He didn't know how to react. He had never seen his father this way. Up close the strong face looked waxy, the body rigid.

"Dad, what is it?"

"Nothing, son."

Garrett didn't believe it. Something was wrong. Clarence retired to his room. After cleaning up the kitchen, Garrett waited at his desk until his father came to say good night.

"It's almost eleven, Garrett," he said when he came in. "Shouldn't you be asleep?"

"I'm not really tired."

Clarence approached the desk and peered over his shoulder. "Where did you get that?"

62

Garrett looked down at the blurred black-and-white photograph, the one with the strange parallel lines and the grainy stamp he couldn't identify. He'd almost forgotten about it. "I found it in the hall closet. Remember, I told you I'd been using your camera equipment. You didn't object. I was going to ask you what the photo was."

Clarence picked up the print gingerly. "It's part of my work, Garrett. You know I can't tell you too much. It's not terribly significant. Some reject that got left behind."

Garrett pretended not to notice as his father slid the photo in his jacket pocket. It didn't feel like a reject.

"Can't you give me a hint?" Garrett prodded. "I was curious about the image in the background. . . . Is it some kind of stamp?"

"The photo comes from our high-speed photography work in Korea. I shouldn't even tell you that much. Now, Mr. Curious, it's time for bed."

"Dad—are you sure you're okay?" he changed subjects. "Something's on your mind—"

"Maybe, but I'll be fine."

Garrett tried to anticipate, but it wasn't the right time to ask. He knew his father well enough. There were times he talked nonstop, others when he withdrew into himself. Garrett put on pajamas and slid between the cool sheets. The phone rang almost immediately. Five minutes later it jangled again. His father answered from his bedroom. In half an hour Garrett counted seven incoming calls.

The next thing he heard was Clarence stirring at his desk in the living room, rustling papers. A briefcase kept snapping open and shut. Finally the garage door shuttered open, and the car coughed and whined as it came to life.

Garrett switched on his bedside lamp. Why hadn't his father told him where he was going? He peered at his watch. It was after midnight. Was this an emergency? He didn't know whether he was more worried or annoyed by Clarence's secrecy, as he padded down the hall and into Clarence's bedroom. His father usually kept any messages by his phone.

A breeze wafted through a half-open window, yet everything felt still and oppressive. At its heart the smallish room was as spartan and practical as Garrett's—a single bed, table, bureau, a lot of books—but somehow it felt different. A shelf across from the bed was now laden with his father's purchases from Korea. Ancient ceramic bowls. Religious artifacts. Delicate porcelain figurines.

There was nothing on the pad by the phone. Frustrated, Garrett searched under the bed, in the closet, behind the desk. Crazy—what did he think he would find?

He fought to keep his imagination from taking control. Everything would be fine. Back in his room his head dropped on his pillow, but his eyes focused stonily on the ceiling. Two hours passed before the garage door creaked open. Clarence moved into the house with steps so light that Garrett strained to hear.

There was no point in confronting his father, he convinced himself, because there was nothing wrong, nothing to worry about anymore. Clarence was back from wherever the emergency had taken him. Whatever the crisis, it was over. There was no one more self-reliant or capable than his father. Garrett had all the faith in the world.

10

Faith meant very little, Garrett saw at breakfast the next morning. His father, puffy-eyed and unshaven, looked as if he hadn't slept in a week. He barely glanced at Garrett, and he didn't talk much. Usually he was dressed and off to the office by now. Maybe the mystery of last night wasn't quite over. Garrett pushed away his cereal bowl.

"Are you going to tell me what's going on or not?" He broke the silence. "I heard you go out last night."

Clarence's proud face swung up. He looked caught off-guard, and troubled again.

"Dad—"

"I appreciate your concern, Garrett. But this is none of your business."

"What's not my business? Look, you asked me to be more responsible. I'm trying to be—I'm trying to help you—but you have to give me some clue about the problem."

Clarence shifted in his chair. "All I can tell you, son, is the world is not always a friendly place."

"What's that supposed to mean?"

"You're going to be late for school. And you have a football game to be thinking about. I'll try to be there—"

"Who cares about school!"

"All right, Garrett," he said, crossing his arms over his chest. He seemed to disappear into himself, gathering his thoughts. "You really want to know?"

"Of course I want to know! I care about you. . . ." He didn't mean to sound so alarmed, or meddlesome. Maybe his father hardly needed the same attention as his mother had—maybe he didn't need help at all—but Garrett wanted to be involved.

"In my line of work," Clarence said after a beat, "there are certain dangers."

Garrett's mouth opened. "Dangers?"

"These are things I normally don't discuss with outsiders."

"What dangers?" Garrett insisted. "And I'm not an outsider—"

"There are some people who want to hurt me."

"What?"

"I know that sounds crazy and out of the blue. I didn't even want to bring it up. I don't want you worried."

"I don't believe you." Garrett squirmed in his chair. "What people? Why?"

"I can't be more specific. I'm sorry. This is another reason I was hesitant to invite you to Los Angeles. It wasn't just my frequent traveling. But I'd hoped by now the trouble would have blown over."

"Dad, you have to do better. I need to know—"

"I can't do any better, Garrett. Quentin and I are privy to some very sensitive military information. Over time, certain parties have threatened us in order to learn those secrets. I've always lived with the possibility of harm, but I also know how to take care of myself. My deepest concern," he said, "is that no one bothers you."

Garrett's heart accelerated. "Bother me? Why would anyone do that?"

"Have you ever been followed?" Clarence asked.

"No." It was like his father was talking in riddles, playing some game. No one had followed him, not that he was aware of.

"Dad, what's so special about your work? You're an aerospace engineer—like a lot of people in your plant. Is everyone in danger? Or does this have to do with your high-speed photography? What about that print I found in the closet?"

"You're asking too many questions. Things will be all right. You have to trust me."

Garrett rolled his eyes in frustration.

"Son, do you trust me?"

"You know I do," he said, but he was still upset.

"If you want to be responsible, concentrate on your schoolwork. Just tell me if anything out of the ordinary occurs. Be especially careful about trusting anyone you don't know. Do you understand?"

No, he thought, he understood almost nothing, except that his father was in some kind of danger. Clarence didn't want to continue the discussion. Garrett picked up his books and left the house reluctantly.

In class his thoughts ran in a million different directions. He called home after lunch and let the phone ring. With the same futility he tried Quentin's home, and his father's number at the aerospace company. Where was everyone? Suited up for the game, he was still agitated as he dropped next to Cleeb on the bench.

"You look like you're having a stroke. It's just a football game," Cleeb said as the refs convened on the field with the two captains. "Don't be so uptight."

"Who's uptight?" But Garrett heard the crossness in his voice. It was too much to explain. Cleeb gave him a funny look as Garrett kept scanning the crowded bleachers.

"Who are you looking for?" he finally inquired with his lopsided grin. "Some lovely young thing I should know about?"

"Funny."

67

"Then who?"

"My father."

"Don't sweat it. My dad always promises to come but never does. 'Doctors are very busy people,' he tells me afterward. You get used to it."

"That's not it," Garrett said. His frustration was boiling over. He looked at Cleeb, and then he hesitated. Don't trust anyone you don't know, Clarence had said. How well did he know Cleeb?

"I'm worried about my dad," Garrett volunteered anyway. He had to tell someone.

"What are you worried about?"

"He's acting strange. Like someone's after him."

Cleeb gave his patented smirk. "Murchinson, good buddy, for someone who says he doesn't watch TV, you've got a flair for the dramatic. You make it sound like a bunch of gangsters are lurking in the shadows. Is your father a mobster? Gimme a break. Maybe you haven't been getting enough sleep."

"Yeah, maybe." Maybe his imagination was taking over. Where was his control, anyway? He thought of the Masters of the Universe.

With the kickoff he turned his attention to the game, but he couldn't concentrate. By the second quarter the score was tied at fourteen when he felt Cleeb's elbow. Coach Enderbee's bony finger was raised in Garrett's direction.

The field felt as long as a supertanker as he trotted toward the huddle. He was already out of breath.

"Sixteen wide body, Murchinson left end sweep. On zero-twenty," the quarterback hissed. Garrett nodded, though he couldn't believe this was his chance. The coach had faith in him; the whole team did. *I'm not ready*, Garrett said, but the words locked in his throat.

The quarterback pitched him the ball. For a moment Garrett felt invulnerable. His legs responded; the adrenaline overwhelmed his system. He eluded one tackle and shot around the line of scrimmage. He saw himself accelerating, sweeping toward the end zone, his father standing between the goal posts with his hands raised in triumph.

Something struck from behind. Pain shot up his spinal column and fanned through his shoulder blades. His legs flew out from under him. How could he suddenly be on the ground? He didn't comprehend as a frenzied roar erupted from the stands. Garrett pushed himself up to see the fumbled ball in the arms of the opposing linebacker. The boy had scrambled back to the Wilshire forty.

Face burning, Garrett trotted to the sidelines. His eyes pointed straight ahead. Squeezed into the first row of bleachers was Clarence. Where had he come from? Relief washed over Garrett that his father was fine, but after a moment he only felt more humiliation. How could he have screwed up in front of his dad?

In the third quarter Enderbee ordered him back on the battlefield. *I'm fine now, I'll do better, I won't fail,* he thought as he listened to the whispered commands of the quarterback. He pushed away all his fear and doubts. He knew he was a Master of the Universe.

The huddle broke with a clap of hands. Garrett darted to his left and took the bad pass at his shoelaces. Three quick steps and he had enough daylight to gallop eight yards before he was tackled. Cheers rang in his ears.

On the next play he swept the other end. A kamikaze cornerback plowed into his left side like a Mack truck. The ball catapulted from Garrett's arms. *Just like that,* he thought, splayed on the ground. He couldn't believe it. What had happened to all his faith, his control? He wanted to die.

"Two fumbles, what a bitch," Adam commiserated when the game ended. Garrett didn't listen. Wilshire had lost by a touchdown, and he held himself responsible. He wanted his teammates to blame him. He wanted to quit. Instead, in the swirling steam of the locker room, understanding looks fell around him. Cleeb reminded him again of the party tonight, victory or no victory.

"Hey, there're a billion people in India," he added.

69

"Do you think any of them gives a damn about what happened at Wilshire Academy today?"

"I screwed up."

"Right. And it hurts. I know—I've been there. Next time you'll do better."

"I don't need a pep talk."

"Too bad," Cleeb said. "I'm giving it anyway. Now cheer up, okay?"

It took Garrett forever to shower and dress. He was the last out of the gym, but his father was still waiting on the field. The handsome face didn't look as preoccupied as it had this morning. Maybe the emergency, whatever it was, was really over this time. Replacing the worry, a light of determination shone in Clarence's eyes. Garrett envied the control and poise his father possessed. Garrett felt like slinking under the door to his room and never coming out.

"What happened out there, son?"

"Bad day, I guess."

"Bad days don't just happen," his father said in his even voice as they strolled to the car. "They're made. You weren't concentrating. Your mind was a million miles away."

Garrett shrugged as if the afternoon meant nothing, but his father's words hurt.

"You have to learn to focus. You won't succeed at the big things until you master the little."

"Yes, sir."

"Don't you want to make me proud of you?"

Of course I want you to be proud, but I screwed up partly because I was worried about you, Garrett thought. *And what about the one play I did right? Didn't you see that?* Garrett looked away from his father for a moment. He wished Clarence wasn't so judgmental. Garrett felt defeated and he couldn't remember his mother's words about his father. Was Clarence the person he thought his father to be, or was he more complex and difficult?

All he could think about now was escaping. "Is it okay

70

if I go out tonight?" he asked at the car. "There's this little party."

Clarence started the engine. "I don't think so, son."

"You don't think what?"

"I don't want you to go," he answered calmly.

"Listen, most of the team will be there. I really want to go." Was his father handing out a punishment for not focusing on the game? Garrett couldn't believe it.

"Parties are a waste of time. Just like television or video games. Or buying fashionable clothes."

"That's not fair," Garrett said. Resentment rushed through him. His father sounded so high-handed. Didn't he see how bad Garrett felt already?

"Remember when we talked about values, Garrett?"

"What about them?"

"I'm trying to teach you to use your time judiciously."

Garrett clucked his tongue. What did his father think, that Garrett's ideals and standards would be corrupted forever if he went to one party?

At home he headed directly to his room, but Clarence called him back. Garrett stood at his door. He didn't want to hear yet another speech about values. He'd refuse to listen.

"I want to show you something." Clarence's voice filled the silence. "Something very important."

His curiosity moved him a few cautious steps toward his father. Clarence stood over the briefcase on the dining table.

"First, I can see you're upset, and I think I owe you an apology."

"For what?" Garrett said casually, even though he felt that an apology was definitely due him. His father's face had turned conciliatory.

"Last night, when I told you the photograph you found meant nothing? I wasn't being candid. And this morning, I know I alarmed you. That wasn't fair. Maybe those things affected your concentration."

"It's okay. I know your job means secrecy."

"Yes," he said, looking slightly troubled again, "but I have decided to make you privy to some information. You must promise not to tell a soul anything—"

"I promise." Garrett didn't know which was his stronger reaction, anxiety or excitement. His father was going to take him into his confidence. That's what he'd always wanted. He watched as Clarence retrieved a legal-size manila envelope from his briefcase and dumped black-and-white photos on the table. Each showed virtually the same image—a series of parallel, close-knit lines that made absolutely no sense to Garrett. Peering closer, he realized that the prints weren't quite identical. In some the lines were closer together, or a little longer, or slightly blurred. In the middle, running through the lines, was a small, dark, round smudge.

"Are the photos from a streak camera?" Garrett asked.

Clarence nodded. "Exactly. From one of the cameras in the closet."

"You didn't mind me looking at the cameras, did you?" Garrett asked, to be reassured.

"Not at all. Curiosity is the foundation of all knowledge," Clarence answered. "As long as you're careful, you can examine the cameras to your heart's content. Just let me know ahead of time." He held up a long, thin thread. Garrett was puzzled as he followed his father to the closet and watched him stretch the thread between one of the cameras and the lip of the shelf, securing it with Scotch tape. The thread was impossible to detect in the grainy light. "You couldn't have known, but you broke this when you took down the cameras."

Garrett was surprised that his father had set a trap. He was impressed that Clarence was oriented to catch a thief. It felt like a ploy from a James Bond movie. Clarence began to talk now about high-speed cameras. Shutter speed. Light. Mechanical versus electronic. Reproduction quality. The advantages and disadvantages of a streak camera. They looked at the prints together.

"What are they of, exactly?" Garrett asked.

"The trajectory of a bullet as it slams into a piece of a special alloy. If you know what you're looking at, the photos tell you both the speed of the projectile and—more importantly—its impact on the alloy. See those symmetrical vertical lines?"

Garrett squinted. He couldn't figure out what they were.

"The lines are the actual metal as it's struck by the bullet, which is that little dark smudge you see. The high-speed camera shows what happens on impact. The alloy's extremely resilient, giving way with the bullet, just enough to trap or repel the projectile without being penetrated by it."

"You mean the camera can actually show all that?" It strained his imagination, almost hurt, to see a bullet slamming, in slow motion, into metal.

"The miracle of high-speed photography. Combine speed with the right lens magnification, Garrett, and there're precious few secrets in the world."

"The streak camera isn't the only one that can show the trajectory of a bullet, is it?" Garrett asked. "The electronic framing camera does it with slightly clearer images."

Clarence looked surprised. "How do you know that?"

"I did some reading at the library." Garrett could see the pleasure and satisfaction in his father's eyes. They mirrored his own.

"The electronic framing camera does exactly what you would think," Clarence explained. "The film used is nothing more than a four-by-five-inch Polaroid negative, the kind you buy at the drugstore. But the high-speed camera is able to print five to ten small images, or frames, on that four-by-five surface. You can follow a sequence of events the naked eye can't apprehend. I once photographed a hummingbird in flight so you could see every lift and downdraft of its wings—wings that move seventy times a second. On film the hummingbird looks like it's standing still."

Garrett picked up one of the photos again. "What kind of alloy is this?"

"Very experimental. Heat-resistant, bullet-resistant, almost impossible to destroy. We're using it on the X-Forty-four plane you saw at the plant, as well as other weaponry. It's something we originally developed with South Korean scientists, but it's the South Koreans who are doing most of the research now. They claim they've actually improved the alloy, made it even stronger and more resilient. We're about to run our own experiments in our lab here. We want to see for ourselves."

Garrett tried to comprehend all that had happened as he sat on the sofa. "This is what you do when you go to Korea? You work on testing this special metal for the plane?"

"Something like that."

He cocked his head. "Is this the secret someone's after?"

Clarence hesitated.

"Who's after you?" Garrett pushed. "Why? Won't you tell me?"

"I've told you enough already, Garrett. I don't want you to worry. The rest you don't need to know."

"But I am worried," he insisted.

"Son, you have to trust my judgment."

"I do"—he raised his voice, more frustrated than ever— "but I don't see why you have to keep things from me." Wasn't it obvious by now that Clarence had *his* complete trust and loyalty? That Garrett didn't like being shut out, that nothing made him crazier? Whatever secrets they did share left Garrett with a good feeling, created a bond between them, and now he wanted to know everything.

"Aren't I your son?" he spoke up. "Aren't you sometimes hard on me because you believe in my special potential? You think I'm different from most boys. I know that. You want to help me live up to my potential because that's what your mother and father never did for you. But how can I do that unless you really show you trust me?"

Garrett stopped. He couldn't believe he was saying this. All his feelings had poured out. His father looked as surprised as he. Clarence took the photos and carefully sealed the manila envelope.

"All right, Garrett. You want me to prove you have my trust? Are you doing anything special tomorrow?"

"Saturday? I don't think so." He'd planned to use the weekend to finish his history paper.

"Sometime before noon, take your regular bus route to school, but get off at Sunset and Melrose. Drop the envelope at this address." He penciled the number at the top. "It won't take you long."

"Who do I give it to?"

"You're going to an apartment complex. There's a mail slot in the first door on your right. One of my colleagues lives there."

"First door on the right," he repeated. It was hard to hide his pleasure. All the anger and frustration of the afternoon was gone.

"You're a good boy. I want you to know that," Clarence said. "I want you to know I could never be more proud of anyone." Leaning over, his father seemed bigger than life as he kissed Garrett on the cheek.

11

"I'm afraid Korea beckons again. Quentin and I have to leave first thing tomorrow."

Garrett turned off the hose by the apple tree. Clarence looked apologetic for the sudden news, but Garrett wasn't bothered. He would miss his father, but he would show him he could be responsible in his absence. No more late movies or beer drinking this time.

In the house, the Sunday paper was spread over the living room sofa, the only thing out of place. As usual, Clarence had read the *Times* page by page. Garrett knew there wasn't a day his father couldn't tell him what was happening in the world.

"When will you be back?" Garrett asked.

"Within a week."

"Do you want to leave a hotel number?"

"There's no point. I'll be traveling a lot. You sure you'll be okay?"

"Of course."

While his father packed, Garrett got busy on his history paper. He had proposed his own theories for class economic differences that he wanted Clarence to read. The gap between rich and poor seemed almost a historic certainty. The rich perpetuated their wealth for the next generation and had no real interest in sharing it with the poor. He had only to look at the kids at his school. A few were involved in civic projects like helping the homeless, but the majority cared mostly about material things. Garrett wondered how he would characterize himself. Hadn't he bought an entire new wardrobe? Hadn't he admitted to himself he wouldn't mind owning a car like Cleeb's? Whose side was he on?

Garrett's head shot up. His father was leaning against the wall by the bed, as if he'd materialized out of nowhere. There was another legal-size manila envelope under his arm.

"Can you help me out again, Garrett?"

"While you're away? Sure, you know I can."

Garrett took the sealed envelope and placed it on his desk. Yesterday he'd dropped off his father's package without a hitch. No one had followed, despite vague fears in the back of his mind. There had been no danger whatsoever. "Same place?" he asked.

"No," Clarence said. "There's a drive-in movie theater on Victory. My colleague will meet you at the concession stand after school tomorrow. The theater's on the way to his house. You must be there by four-thirty, not a minute later."

"Four-thirty? I can't, Dad. I've got practice."

"I'm sorry to interrupt your schedule," he said sympathetically, "but life doesn't come without some conflicts. You have to decide what's more important to you, Garrett— football or helping me. Didn't you tell me you wanted my complete trust?"

"I do, but can't this wait until five-thirty or six?"

His father turned and left him in silence.

The end of fifth period Garrett paced in front of the trophy case, waiting for Cleeb and Adam. The three

77

usually walked over to practice together, but after a few seconds Garrett wheeled around and headed out the side door. He hesitated on the steps, then went straight off campus. It bothered him to be missing practice, but this was his first time. He had a more important responsibility this afternoon. He hadn't been sure how he was going to handle this conflict. But now it was clear. He wasn't going to let his father down. Tomorrow he'd give the coach an excuse. It wasn't the end of the world, was it?

The bus took him to the public library. It was less than a fifteen-minute walk to the drive-in on Victory, so he had some time. The book on high-speed photography was exactly where Garrett had left it, marker and all. It took all his concentration to understand laser diodes. The average power and duty cycle was low for the short, high-power pulses. For use in backlighting and shadow-graphy, semiconductor diodes could provide enough energy to expose conventional infrared film, but they had several disadvantages when used as a pulsed light source—they couldn't sustain themselves over long periods.

He made sure he left the library by four. The drive-in, as Garrett half expected, was closed, but slipping through the gate and finding the concession stand was a cinch. He thought some early-arriving employee might be around. As Garrett stood self-consciously at the concession counter, his eyes darted back and forth.

At a quarter to five he was still waiting. His father had been insistent on being punctual. Had the colleague screwed up, or had he? Maybe there was a second drive-in on Victory. Garrett hadn't thought to ask Clarence for more explicit instructions. His father would be disappointed. Did Garrett dare just leave the package? What were the photos being used for? He assumed there were photographs in the envelope.

It was easier than he thought to unstick the tape. He worked carefully so no one would know he'd tampered with the envelope. His hand reached in to pull out the photos, when several bulky sheets of paper, neatly folded,

78

slid out instead. Opened, he saw blueprints that looked like a maze, with details so fine, Garrett had no idea what they represented. He pushed them back and resealed the tape.

He waited until after six and reluctantly left with the envelope. Every few yards he walked, Garrett spun around, hoping his father's colleague might somehow recognize him and claim the blueprints. There was no one on the crowded sidewalk who looked even remotely interested.

His consternation deepened as the bus took him home. Should he revisit the drive-in tomorrow? Or maybe his father's associate would call. Why hadn't Clarence at least given him a name? Why hadn't Garrett had the foresight to ask for one?

On foot, approaching his own block, he stopped abruptly. A short, wispy Asian man in a Hawaiian shirt was on the sidewalk, directly in front of his house. Garrett eyed him suspiciously. He had never seen the stranger in the neighborhood. The hard, angular face was unsettling, and when the man suddenly turned and stared at Garrett, he felt a chill. Before Garrett could study him more closely, the man vanished around the corner.

Garrett unlocked and entered his house. In his mind's eye, he could still see the Asian man. Something about him was eerie. Garrett stood uncertainly in the hallway, and in the kitchen he felt even more uncomfortable. Hadn't he left the phone next to the refrigerator? What was it doing on the counter? Checking his father's room, he found the door ajar. Nothing seemed out of place inside, but he couldn't be positive. In his own room, which he knew best, two desk drawers had been left open a crack.

He peered into the hall closet and let his eyes climb to the row of cameras. Everything seemed in place, but he moved his fingers along the shelf anyway.

One end of the thread was still taped to the edge; the other was on the carpet.

His pulse quickened. There had been no signs of forced

entry into the house, yet he knew the locks on the rear windows didn't work. He remembered Clarence's warning about being followed. The Asian hadn't exactly followed Garrett, but had he broken into the house? Garrett felt certain someone had. He toyed with calling the police. What could they possibly do? What proof did he have? Garrett found himself staring out the living room window as evening shadows rippled over the yard.

He needed to talk to someone just to get a sane opinion. He thought of calling Cleeb, but his father had told him everything in confidence. All this was *their* secret. His thoughts traveled back to the hidden thread. Who knew his father had those cameras? Why weren't they kept at the aerospace company? Surely that was the most secure place. After today Garrett didn't think they were safe at the house. Whatever the blueprints showed, maybe they weren't safe, either. Then it occurred to Garrett that the Asian may have been looking for the blueprints.

He retreated to his room and sat on a corner of his bed. His pulse kept racing. Garrett hated it when he panicked. He hated anxiety and uncertainty. He had to stay calm, think this out. Pulling himself up, he retrieved the cameras from the closet. He placed everything in a deep cardboard box, including the blueprints, then grabbed the car keys. There was a Greyhound bus station not too far away, he thought as he drove. His eyes kept skating to the rearview mirror. When he felt sure no one was following, he parked and walked as casually as he could inside the station. He placed everything in a locker, shoveling the bus key to the bottom of his jeans pocket. He didn't think he was being paranoid. His resourcefulness was something his father would be proud of.

He had nothing to be afraid of, he thought. Whoever had broken into the house wouldn't come back when Garrett was home. Still, his hands weren't exactly steady as he steered the car into the garage. The door to the house squeaked open. He'd left the lights on, and he slipped down the hallway, opening doors. He entered the kitchen, where he noted nothing had been disturbed.

80

Safe, he thought with relief, but almost before he caught his breath the phone shrilled.

Garrett let it ring for almost a minute before reluctantly picking it up.

The clicks started softly, sounding like someone running his thumb over the teeth of a comb. A deep buzzing sound followed, and finally a gentle hum. They were the same sounds he'd heard when he'd picked up the calls during his father's first trip to Korea. Someone was on the other end; Garrett was sure of it.

"Who is this?" he demanded. He felt silly, yet he knew he wasn't talking to himself. "Who are you? What do you want?"

When no one answered, he hung up and locked the door to his room.

12

The ball sailed over his shoulder, fat and oval like a flying saucer, into his outstretched arms. *A gift*, thought Garrett, *an opportunity*. Two linebackers collapsed on him, but Garrett was a step quicker; after the season opener he was also wiser. He accelerated to a gear no one could touch, and his arms stuck to the ball like glue. He glided into the end zone. The roar from the bleachers carried onto the field like a sweet melody. Why couldn't his father be here?

"Hero material," Cleeb said sincerely when the game ended. An arm looped around Garrett, then another, and another. The prisoner could barely breathe until he reached the locker room.

"Thanks," he whispered. Two touchdowns. Maybe one day he'd deserve to be a starter.

"Let's get out of here," Adam said when the three were dressed. "There's a kung fu movie at the Lensic."

Garrett pretended he had to retie his shoes, but he could feel Cleeb's stare.

"Not again, Murchinson," Cleeb moaned when Garrett finally straightened and made eye contact.

"Look, I'm sorry. I'm busy tonight—"

"First you miss my party," Adam interrupted, "then you won't go along with the plague joke. What kind of Masters of the Universe member are you?"

Cleeb shook his head. "And don't tell us about homework on a Friday night. You're getting straight A's. Did you know that even Einstein was a notorious drunk who chased women on weekends?"

"Guys, it's my father. He's coming home." Garrett tried to look innocent, but he didn't think Cleeb was impressed.

"So? My old man travels a lot, too. He doesn't care if I'm home when he shows. What's so special? Is your father still being chased by gangsters?"

"Right, gangsters," Garrett joked, but he felt his face warm. He didn't want to talk about it. He had too many questions of his own.

"What's your old man do, anyway?" asked Cleeb.

"Aerospace engineer."

"Space-age stuff?"

"You could say that."

"Is that why you can't be a couple hours late? You get zapped by a laser gun?"

Quick laughs all around. Garrett relaxed a little. *Why not take a chance?* he thought. What difference did it make if he went out just one night, or got home a little late? But Clarence had sent a telegram with his arrival time. *Friday, October 13, six P.M.* Garrett knew it wasn't only a matter of meeting his father's expectations. The strangeness of the week had him on edge. He had done a lot of thinking. He wanted some answers right away.

"I don't know about your father," Cleeb said sincerely, "but lately you're the one who's been acting strange. It feels like you're holding something back. Are you okay? Come on, we're friends—"

Garrett cut his eyes away. "Everything's fine," he said.

83

"It's none of our business," Adam interjected, "but with your father, it's like he has this power over you."

"What are you talking about? My father's strict, but he doesn't run my life."

"Don't get uptight. Look, my old man is a royal pain, too," Adam admitted.

"My father isn't like yours," Garrett corrected him.

"Yeah? How's he so different?"

Cleeb shot his friend a look. "Hey, Adam, lay off. There's no accounting for family. If Murchinson says his dad's different, he's different, okay?" He turned to Garrett, trying to make peace. "You going to come to the dance next Wednesday? You can meet all those Winchester girls you missed at our party."

"I'll be there."

"You're sure?" Adam prodded. "Maybe by then we can think of a new Masters of the Universe stunt."

"I promise," he said, relieved to end the discussion. "You can count on me."

Cleeb and Adam nodded as if they believed him, but Garrett knew they were disappointed about this evening. There had been another phone call last night, the third in a row, with the same strange clicking and humming. Finally Garrett had left the receiver off the hook. He tried to convince himself the calls were just pranks, but he didn't quite believe it.

A pair of headlights swept into Garrett's driveway. Half asleep, he bolted from the couch. It was after midnight. Why was his father so late? He realized he could have gone with Cleeb and Adam and been home with time to spare.

In the shadows of the porch light Garrett opened the door for his father. Clarence looked pasty white, and his eyes were red. Quentin wasn't with him. In the living room, Clarence unlatched his suitcase. No presents this time, Garrett saw, only rumpled clothes, and a case from

84

which his father delicately extracted the electronic framing camera. Clarence opened the closet before Garrett had thought to tell him what had happened.

"What have you done? Where are the cameras?" he asked in his even voice.

Garrett feared he had done the wrong thing and began to explain. He felt like he was confessing. His father's colleague had not met him at the drive-in. Returning home, he'd seen a stranger near the house. The thread protecting the cameras had been broken. Later there were strange phone calls. He had been scared, and worried. Wasn't it intelligent to want to hide the cameras and the blueprints? Garrett lifted the bus locker key from his pocket.

"How do you know about the blueprints?" Clarence asked.

"I looked in the envelope." He didn't want to lie to his father. "I know you didn't want me to, but I was worried when your colleague didn't show. Dad, I did what I thought was right."

His father began pacing the room. Garrett had never seen him so agitated. Clarence fired questions at Garrett. Exactly what did the stranger look like? Was he an Asian, short and slight, cold- and hard-looking? Would it have been obvious to the man that Garrett was carrying something? How long did the phone calls last? Describe the sound on the other end in detail.

"It was a clicking noise, then a hum. Like a long-distance connection," Garrett answered the last question, bewildered that his father could describe the stranger so accurately.

"Was this the first time you received a call like that?"

"No. I may have forgotten to tell you, but on your first trip it happened, too. Twice, on the same night."

"What you were experiencing wasn't long-distance static, Garrett. The calls came from quite close by. What you heard was a piece of sophisticated electronics. You were

85

not just being recorded, your voice was being analyzed. Remember when I told you about voice prints?"

Garrett's lips parted. Was his father kidding? "A voice print? Of me? Why would someone want that?"

His father seemed preoccupied again as he lifted the car keys from the table. "Maybe we should go for a ride," he said.

13

"Where are we going? What's so urgent? Dad. you're exhausted, it's so late. . . ."

He watched as his father started the car. The cool night air wrapped around Garrett as if nothing were out of the ordinary.

"Get in," Clarence said from the rolled-down window.

The emphatic tone belied his father's bloodshot eyes and bent shoulders. Garrett slammed the car door shut. He noticed another manila envelope on the seat between them.

"So, what is it?" Garrett asked as his father drove silently.

"I'm afraid I'm in some rather serious trouble." His father's large hands gripped the steering wheel as the car swung off the freeway. The side artery had no streetlights.

"You mean someone is still out to hurt you? You already told me—"

"Yes, I told you. And at the time you wanted to know

more because you didn't understand. But now I think you do understand. At least some of it."

"Understand what?" Garrett said evasively.

"You have a lot of questions, don't you?"

Yes, he thought, *plenty.*

"You also already know some of the answers."

The beads of sweat gathered on Garrett's face, his neck, skimmed down his ribs. "I think something strange is going on," he admitted.

"You think more than that."

"Okay," he said, "maybe I do."

"You think I'm doing something wrong, something illegal."

Garrett couldn't look at his father. He wasn't sure what he believed, but he had suspicions. "I don't know. Yeah, sometimes I do. I get worried. Strange photos, and then blueprints, the way you hide things. The secret deliveries I make for you. Is this all really part of your job? When you go to Korea on company business, the high-speed cameras aren't part of it, are they? They belong to you and Quentin. That's why you keep everything at home instead of at the plant. I mean, your company is working on that jet fighter, and maybe it's studying that special alloy along with the Koreans, but you and Quentin take those photos on your own time, don't you? For what? Who wants them? Somebody does, because I think that's why our house was broken into. . . ."

Garrett turned to face his father. "Who's the Asian man?"

Clarence looked anxious, then relieved, then upset again. Garrett knew that his theory, intricate and crazy as it sounded, must be right. He sensed his father was proud of him for being perceptive. Only Garrett wasn't proud. He felt like he was sinking in some hole.

"Are you going to tell me, or not?" Garrett demanded.

"The man's name is Chou Do Li," Clarence said quietly as he kept driving. "He's a citizen of the Democratic

People's Republic of Korea. In a tribute to euphemisms and self-deception, that's what North Korea calls itself. Chou is more than a citizen—he's a government official. He has also decided to be my personal enemy. I've been afraid of him breaking into my house for months. You were smart to move the cameras, Garrett. Chou wouldn't risk taking them—that would be too obvious, and it's the photos he's really after—but your instincts were right."

Garrett tried to feel good about the praise, but his head was swimming. "I don't understand. This Chou, why's he your enemy? What's he want with the photos?"

"I'm afraid that now he's your enemy, too, Garrett."

"My enemy?" he exclaimed.

"Chou knows you live with me. What he doesn't know is whether you're involved in my work. The voice recordings he made are the start of an attempt to learn everything he can about you."

"What work? What are you saying?" Garrett's questions couldn't keep up with his thoughts.

"You'll have to excuse me, Garrett, for not being more honest in the beginning, but I couldn't take that chance. Now things have gotten out of hand. It's only right I tell you the truth. The first drop you made, at the apartment house, was legitimate. Then I began to worry if Chou really was on to you. So I staged the next one, at the drive-in."

"Staged? You mean it was all meaningless?"

"The blueprints were meaningless—the mechanical system of Los Angeles City Hall. That was in case Chou somehow got hold of the envelope. But he didn't follow you. Which means he doesn't know you're helping me. That's what I needed to find out. That part wasn't meaningless at all."

"Wait. Slow down," Garrett said. He dropped his head back on the seat. His father was making this up. But when Garrett took in Clarence's grim expression there was nothing make-believe about it. "Dad, you don't know how

89

absurd this sounds. Nothing makes sense. You said I was helping you—with what?"

"I know you're brighter than that, Garrett. And you aren't naive. This all makes perfect sense. You must have guessed my real work by now."

"I don't know anything," he said stubbornly. His face and neck were moist.

"Then let me be crystal clear," his father said with new urgency. "Chou has been dogging me for several months. He would like to know exactly what I do when I go to Seoul. South Korea is the enemy of his homeland."

I want to know, too, thought Garrett, but suddenly he wasn't sure. He had a sense of danger again. How had he gotten involved in all this?

"I work for a special agency of the United States government," Clarence continued. "That's who owns the cameras. A little-known branch of military intelligence, even though, technically, I'm a civilian. My work involves industrial espionage in foreign countries."

"Espionage?" Garrett didn't recognize his voice. "What are you saying—you're a spy?" Garrett fought off a laugh. "A spy? You're not a spy. Dad. . . ." His eyes glided over his father again. Spies wore trench coats and dark glasses, didn't they? Of course, Garrett had never seen or known a spy except in books or movies. How well did he know Clarence? He remembered bragging to Monroe that he might have been separated from his father for ten years but somehow he still understood him. Maybe he understood very little.

"Is this all true?" Garrett whispered.

"Why do you think I've lived in half a dozen cities and worked for so many companies the last decade? I'm assigned, Garrett, by our government. They find me the jobs. With my aerospace training I can be of invaluable service, going overseas on the pretext of working for some company. I've done espionage work in Germany, Egypt, England, Greece, Pakistan. This is a complex world.

Sometimes there're dangers the public doesn't see or understand—technical things even the CIA doesn't get involved with—and it's my job and Quentin's to bring back very specific engineering information on sensitive projects."

"You mean your aerospace company doesn't know you do this?"

"It doesn't have a whiff. My job's just a cover."

"Then the colleague I dropped off the photos to—he's not an aerospace employee? He works for the government?"

"Yes."

"What are the photos of exactly? Why are they so valuable to Chou?"

"That part you already know. The photos show bullet trajectories and their impact on the special alloy that we and the South Koreans are developing. What's different among the photos is the kinds of bullets used in the tests. We're experimenting with different weapons, just to prove how effective this metal is. Chou probably has some data on the alloy, but the photos provide him visual proof of its strength."

"I don't get this at all." Garrett blew out the corner of his mouth. "Why are you spying on South Korea? It's one of our allies."

"The sad truth is, ally or not, South Korea doesn't always share its research with us, and we like to know what our supposed friends are doing. No one can be totally trusted, Garrett. Believe me, it's not easy going to Seoul on company business and then furtively setting up cameras at night in the Koreans' labs."

Garrett fought off his shock. His father worked for some branch of the U.S. government. How long had this been going on? "This Chou," he said, "how does he know what you're doing?"

"There was a leak. The North Koreans have their own spies, both in Seoul and in the States."

"But why doesn't your own agency help you?"

"There's little it can do. I'm on my own. It's always

91

been that way. If I'm caught, if the North Koreans or Chou can prove I'm a spy, our government has to deny it."

"How can that be? Doesn't the government feel any loyalty—"

"One day you'll understand," Clarence said succinctly.

Garrett was dismayed. He had to understand this now, he had to stay in control. "So Chou wants your information, your photos, because South Korea is an enemy of the North."

"And my job now is to see he doesn't get anything."

"You think the man really is dangerous?"

"You saw him. Physically, he's slight and unprepossessing, but if you ever look into his eyes. . . . I know he's fearless. He'll tail me in broad daylight without thinking twice."

Garrett had no difficulty recalling his face. He still felt a chill.

"Chou has no scruples, Garrett. This is a very rough business. If he ever gets the photos from me or Quentin, we're of no more use to him. We're expendable."

"Expendable?" The word sounded strange, as if his father were talking about someone on the football team who wasn't quite good enough.

"You understand what I'm saying, Garrett?"

"What you mean," he breathed, "is he would kill you."

"I have no doubt. I can't prove it, but I'm sure the man and his friends have killed before."

Garrett couldn't talk. How could his father have become a spy? Were ordinary people spies? How was he so calm now? Garrett felt so anxious, he didn't think he could eat or sleep. Well, nothing was going to happen to his father. He wouldn't let it. He had already lost his mother. He would not lose his father. He wouldn't lose control of his life again.

"I've lived with the possibility of violence for a large part of my life," Clarence said. "Starting in Vietnam.

92

Maybe being exposed as a spy was inevitable. But I'll find a way out. I don't want you to worry."

Not worry? He knew his father was resourceful, but what could he do to escape Chou? "Is Quentin in jeopardy, too?"

"Yes."

"How long have you two been spies together?"

"I recruited Quentin after we met at the Helsinki conference. It wasn't long after the military first approached me. Somebody high up knew of my war record and thought once a hero, always a hero. I had just left you and your mother in Arkansas. At first I didn't want anything more to do with the military, but my new aerospace job was so mundane, so boring, that the spy work had appeal. I like being challenged, Garrett, and I saw a chance to accomplish something positive in this world."

Fatigue was spreading through Garrett, but his mind worked feverishly. "I don't understand something. The Helsinki conference, that was on world peace, wasn't it? Do you really believe in that? You and Quentin, you speak out for disarmament, and you told me that after Vietnam you thought our government was a bunch of hypocrites and liars. Then why do you work for it as a spy?"

"Our government *is* hypocritical on many levels, but not all. There are some people, like in the agency I work for, that want to change things for the better. There're a few of us idealists left. The information I gather is used to help keep a balance of world power—that's what we're all after. It's the only sure path to world peace."

Garrett searched in vain for a hole in his father's logic. The car swung onto a road alive with store lights. On the far side of a curve, Clarence rolled to a stop by an all-night convenience mart.

"Stay here," Clarence said softly. He disappeared with the envelope and Garrett watched as he entered the store. When he returned he was carrying the same kind of vinyl attaché case he'd brought home before.

93

"What's in there?" Garrett asked.

"Documents to look at. My government contact left them. And now he has my latest bunch of photos to study." His father put the car in gear and started home. Garrett's shoulders sagged in relief, as if a terrible burden had been lifted, at least for the moment.

Garrett stopped short of asking what the documents were. It didn't matter, did it? He was just amazed by what he'd learned tonight, all this secrecy, and Clarence had made him a part of it. Together, he felt, he and his father could handle the danger. The trust and confidence Clarence had shown were most important. Garrett knew he needed them. Maybe his father knew that, too. Then he began to understand.

"Dad," he said slowly, "you wanted me to figure all this out, didn't you? You know I'm curious by nature. You knew from the first time you told me about the cameras. You saw how interested I was. You knew I'd start asking questions, at least to myself. And the more silent you were, the more I wanted to get involved."

"Go on," Clarence said, listening.

"Now I think I know why you did that. You wanted to see if I would get involved. You thought one day you might need my help, but you didn't want to force me. And when you lectured me about being more responsible, you were really thinking about this. Isn't that right? Then you offered me the job of courier, and I took it."

"Are you angry with me for not being more direct?"

"No. I can see now the pressure you were under. I understand," he said sincerely.

"The end always justifies the means, Garrett." His father seemed to be gathering his thoughts, deliberating on something. Finding fresh strength and energy from a source Garrett could only envy.

"What do you want me to do?" Garrett asked. He could hear the eagerness in his voice. "How can I help you?"

"You can always say no."

"I won't. Just tell me. I'll do anything."

94

"It goes without saying that what happens now is just between you and me. Nobody can know."

"Of course, I understand."

"And as much as you'll have the urge, you can't ask me too many more questions. Particularly about my government contact. I'll inform him you're helping me, but you can't know anything about him. Is that understood, too?"

"Perfectly," Garrett swore.

"Let's stop for a cup of coffee."

14

"Quentin has not been enough help to me lately, Garrett. In fact, he's become a coward. As much as I love my friend, the man has lost his stomach for this pressure. I need your help more than ever."

They sat in a booth at an all-night coffee shop. It was more of a dump than Large Marge's, Garrett thought. The apple pie tasted like cardboard, the fluorescent lights buzzed like insects. Garrett's head kept flicking up to see the night people he would never look twice at during the day—if they were even around—men with waxy mustaches and women in ill-fitting dresses. They looked more like spies than his father. Still, he liked the atmosphere.

"You're saying you can't work with Quentin anymore?" Garrett asked. He felt sad for his father's friend. Quentin's life was a lonely one, and now, if he didn't have Clarence. . . .

"On this last trip I finally let Quentin know. He wouldn't even operate the camera, he was so sure the North Koreans would tell the South Koreans about us. Of course, they won't dare—the North Koreans want us to do their dirty work—but that leaves me to take all the risk. I told you, it's not easy escaping the South Koreans' scrutiny or finding the time to be alone in their defense factories. I go on the pretense of helping them, but still they're suspicious. Doing all this without Quentin's help has become a small hell. That's why I've been so tired lately."

Garrett was confused. "What are you saying? You want me to take Quentin's place? I can't work at the aerospace plant."

"No, but you can help me deceive Chou. I've got a backlog of photos I've yet to deliver. If you can be the courier, you'll take the pressure off me. Despite their strong curiosity, even paranoia, they don't suspect you, Garrett. Why should they? You're just my son, a student who knows nothing about what I do. They'll keep following me and grow tired of my inactivity. You won't have to take my place for long, I promise. Maybe two or three months, and it won't interfere with your life. You can make your drops on the way to and from school."

"You don't think there's any danger?" Garrett asked calmly. His coolness amazed and pleased him.

"Not for you, not right now. If Chou starts to follow, we'll rethink our plan. Garrett, if you're having second thoughts, if you want out, just tell me now. I don't want you to feel pressured or in danger."

"No. No second thoughts. I'm fine," he swore. "But being a spy, all I know about that is from movies, TV. . . ."

"Movies are fantasy," Clarence replied disparagingly.

"So what does a real spy do?"

"There're all kinds, Garrett, most of which I know very little about. My job basically is transmitting information as efficiently as possible. That sounds easy, but it can be challenging. I try never to be reckless or frivolous or needlessly elaborate. My contact and I change locations and times for every drop. We're always aware of who and what is around us. We never talk business on the phone, except in code. We don't attract attention to ourselves."

Garrett nodded, mesmerized, as his father continued.

97

He felt an excitement that wasn't nerves, it was anticipation. He was going to be a spy for his country. If he ever told Adam or Cleeb, they'd probably howl. He'd be accused of inventing another game for Masters of the Universe. But this wasn't a game. This was the real thing. He would have the last laugh. And what would Mr. Fenton say if he knew? Garrett wasn't just going to be studying history anymore, maybe he was going to be a part of it.

"I want you to make a drop this Wednesday," Clarence said. "I'll get things together by tomorrow."

"What kind of things?"

His father eyed him coolly. *If there was something important*, Garrett thought, *Clarence would tell me*. There had to be total trust between them.

Clarence tipped the waitress, and they drove to the bus locker to retrieve the cameras. It was almost three A.M. when they reached home, but Garrett no longer felt an ounce of weariness.

"I have another assignment for you, Garrett," Clarence offered in the house.

"Already?"

"Something in general. I want you to continue reading everything you can about high-speed photography. I'm going to show you how the cameras work. I want you to become as skilled in this field as Quentin was."

"I can do it," he said. He thought, *For my father, I can do anything in the world*.

15

"*Tonight*, to*night* . . .*" trilled the off-key voice.

Garrett started laughing. He tried the combination three times before his hall locker popped open. Grabbing his homework for the evening, he threw another glance at his watch.

". . . won't be just any *night* . . ." Adam kept crooning. His arm slunk around Cleeb's shoulder as the inseparable pair serenaded Garrett out of the building.

"What's your hurry, Murchinson?" Cleeb asked on the steps. "The party doesn't start till eight. And you're twenty billion light-years ahead on your homework."

"Errands to run," Garrett explained, walking backward quickly.

"What gives with the fat smile? You'd think it was your birthday and someone just gave you a Maserati—"

"Maybe something better," Garrett tossed back to Adam. With a wave he sprinted off campus.

He was floating in a special orbit all right. Nothing could dampen his mood. *Talk about everything going your way,* Garrett thought as he reached his bus with half a minute to spare. He took his usual seat in back. His eyes danced over a page of algebra questions before his more important assignment reentered his thoughts. The sealed, unmarked package slipped out of his notebook binder. He had memorized Clarence's instructions for the drop. He would be there exactly on time. He wouldn't disappoint his father.

Garrett studied his reflection in the bus window. Was he really a spy for his country? How he had wanted to confide in Adam and Cleeb, but in the end the secrecy only heightened his exhilaration, and added to his pleasant sense of disbelief. Only a couple of months ago he'd been sitting in a drugstore with his friends in Rainbow. Suddenly he couldn't believe *that* was him. He thought again how he could never go back. He still sometimes missed Monroe and his old friends, but he had outgrown them. That was a different life.

At the corner of Sunset and Gower he began walking five blocks south. He tried not to be obvious when he crossed at the intersections. The package was safely back in his binder, camouflaged, but for a moment it felt as obvious as a suitcase. The early evening traffic seemed to slow deliberately when it passed.

Yet there was nothing to fear, he realized when he reached the shabby, deserted office building being renovated. The construction crew had left for the evening. He was totally alone. The foyer was dusty and filled with debris. As instructed, Garrett placed his package under some boards in the corner and walked away.

He circled the block to make sure he wasn't followed before taking the bus home.

He found Clarence scurrying around the kitchen, fresh and full of energy, the familiar apron tied to his waist. The sweet smell of barbecued steak picked up his appetite. A plate of apples from their tree rested on the counter. Garrett grabbed one.

His father looked up expectantly. "Well?"

Garrett was amused by the tension in his voice. Wasn't

he one hundred percent sure Garrett could handle this challenge? "It was a breeze," he reported. "No problems at all."

"No one followed?"

"Nobody."

"Then congratulations! You did a great job. You must feel proud."

He was proud, Garrett thought as he bit into the apple, but he tried not to show it. That wasn't his nature. "How's everything?" he asked.

"I'm afraid I have some disappointing news," Clarence said as they sat down for dinner. "Quentin quit his job at the aerospace plant this morning."

Garrett put down his fork. "You're kidding. Why?"

"Paranoia. He's not just worried about Chou and the North Koreans. He's afraid our aerospace company is onto him, and he doesn't want anyone to know he's working for the government. Too many complications for his future, he thinks. He wants a clean wash of the spy trade. I told him I understood. This business takes a toll on the nerves."

Garrett thought he could hear some strain even in his father's voice. Yet being a courier didn't bother Garrett. He was sure he could do this forever.

"What's going to happen to Quentin?"

"He'll teach. That's his original profession. He left for New York a few hours ago. Told me to give you his best. He was very fond of you, Garrett."

He regretted that his father's only friend had vanished from their lives. Garrett had liked the warm, soft-spoken man who had been his only other source of information about his father. Clarence didn't seem overly upset. Garrett knew he shouldn't be, either. Life would go on. His father could count on him to fill the void.

"Where are you going?" Clarence called softly when Garrett started to his room.

"I have to put the finishing touches on my history paper, the one I want you to read. It's all on the computer.

101

Then there's a gathering at Cleeb's. Is it okay if I take the car?"

Clarence didn't say a word.

"I'm ahead on my homework," Garrett added to make things clear. He knew his father was antiparty, so he'd fibbed a little. But for Clarence not to let him go out at night wasn't fair.

"Son, I need your help."

"For what?"

"To pick up documents."

"What documents?"

"It can't wait, I'm afraid."

Garrett stared. *Why can't you do this one?* he thought. *I have someplace to go. Everyone's expecting me. I had to cancel last time, and I'm trying to keep my friends at school.*

"Dad," he said, cautiously choosing his words. "I'd like to be able to get out a little bit. You know I'm responsible. Why can't I have some freedom? I'm willing to be your courier, but does it have to be on a moment's notice? I made plans."

"Freedom is wonderful," Clarence replied calmly, "but your work comes first. You say you're responsible, but when you took on this job with me, what about that responsibility? Shouldn't it come ahead of an evening out?"

"You just said I did a great job this afternoon—"

"But the job's not over, Garrett."

"Dad, I know what you're saying, but since you didn't give me any notice. . . ."

"That's the way this business is. I don't get much notice myself. I don't make the rules, Garrett. We're not working in a time-clock situation that's got a schedule. We do what must be done."

"I work hard at school, Dad, and at football. Once in awhile I like some fun, some excitement—"

"Excitement? What could be more of an adventure than being a spy for your country? Son, I realize the gathering

102

is a party. You want to go to the party, fine, go. Then what's best is that you stop helping me altogether. I understand. You don't have the commitment I hoped you had. You're too young. Or maybe you're confused. Maybe you're still thinking about your mother."

"You're wrong, I'm focused. I'm not too young," Garrett countered, annoyed. "It's just that. . . ." His words trailed off. What excuse was he going to make? Either he was in or he was out. If he truly valued helping his father, obviously the party shouldn't be a big deal. Picking up and leaving off documents was part of his job, and it made him feel special and important. He had to have priorities; Clarence had taught him that.

Without telling the truth tomorrow, he'd have to make Cleeb and Adam understand. He thought about calling now to fake being sick, but he decided they'd pressure him to come anyway.

"Okay," he said with a sigh.

"Are you sure, Garrett?"

"Yes, I'm sure. What do I do?"

He drove all the way to Ventura, skirting the ocean and losing his way twice before finding a gas station his father had drawn on a crude map. The trip had taken more than an hour. He arrived a few minutes before ten, relieved to be on time. In the washroom, behind the door, was a briefcase with shiny brass latches.

In the car he hesitated before wedging his cargo under the seat. As a courier, wasn't he entitled to know what he was carrying? His thumb pushed back the latches. *Locked.* He blew out a breath, frustrated, but maybe it was just as well. If Clarence wanted him to know what the documents were, if they were important, he would tell him.

On the freeway Garrett was careful to monitor the traffic. Nobody was tailing him. Certainly the Asian wasn't in view. He wondered if Chou would ever catch on. His foot eased off the accelerator, and he cranked down his window. The sea breeze wafted over him. He had no regrets about missing the party. There'd be others. He

103

thought again how much he liked the night, the sense of a city's sleeping. He felt he could do whatever he wanted without anyone's knowing or getting in his way. A crescent of a moon was shrouded in fog. The cusp seemed to point at him. An omen of luck, Garrett thought. He wished he had one of his father's cameras to take a photo.

Reaching home he was fighting off yawns. He parked in the drive and sauntered up the walkway, peeking into the living room as he dug out his key. Garrett blinked. His father had his back to the window, but Garrett could see a handsomely framed oil painting in his hands. He had never seen it before. Clarence seemed to be admiring it in a way Garrett couldn't define, as if enthralled by its beauty.

"A gift from Quentin," his father explained when Garrett walked in. Clarence held up the painting.

"It's beautiful." Quentin had the same expensive taste as his father. "Here. Everything went without a hitch," and Garrett proudly handed over the briefcase.

16

"Yoo-hoo . . . Mr. Murchinson—"

The burst of laughter brought Garrett out of his daze. Sprawled with the rest of the team on the gym floor, he tried to decipher the pattern of X's and O's on the blackboard.

"You follow Gelber and Morris through the hole at left tackle," the coach repeated to Garrett. "You better pay attention—you're going to start tomorrow."

His embarrassment from the laughter faded. He was going to start? He couldn't believe his dream was happening. With new seriousness he focused on the blackboard, yet after a while his mind began playing tricks. He was wandering down a lightless alley, or hanging out in an unfamiliar park, always looking over his shoulder for Chou, but sure he would never be spotted, sure he would complete his drop. He felt a surge of power, just as he did on the football field. He was a hero who could do whatever he wanted.

When the chalk talk was over, Garrett hurried toward the locker room.

"Hey, wait up."

He turned casually, as if he had no idea what Cleeb wanted.

"You've been avoiding me all day. What's going on?" His friend demanded,

"Nothing."

"And what were you daydreaming about during the chalk talk?"

"Everything's cool," Garrett insisted.

"Yeah? So why did you miss the party?" he asked, the sarcasm growing in his voice. "Your father went out of town again, and you had to drive him to the airport? Or the Mafia is after him, and you had to guard the house with a submachine gun?"

"Come off it," Garrett said, but he could see how annoyed Cleeb was. "I'm more sorry than you that I missed the party. I was going to call you to explain last night. Then something came up. . . . Things are rough at home, but they'll be back to normal soon."

"Sure," Cleeb said, deadpan. "What things?"

Garrett plunked some coins into the soda machine.

"I said, 'What things?' "

I can't tell you, Garrett thought. *Please don't ask*. He stood silently.

"I don't know why you're holding back from me. I'm your friend. You're hiding something. You don't trust me, after Adam and I let you into our secret club. You never invite Adam and me to your house, and you've become secretive about what you do."

"What is this, the third degree? Give me a break."

"Hey, are you in trouble?" Cleeb sounded concerned.

The shift in his friend's voice threw Garrett. Maybe Cleeb really cared. He looked hurt that Garrett wouldn't confide in him. But how could he, even if he was sometimes tempted. He had promised his father.

"Yeah," he finally admitted, taking a swig of soda, "I'm in major trouble. I keep forgetting tomorrow's plays.

106

See ya, okay?" He ducked his head and quickly changed into his clothes. Without saying good-bye to anyone he scampered from the gym.

He was relieved when he reached the library. There was no one to hassle him. He grabbed the familiar reference book and found an empty table.

Conventional flash X ray uses short (few tens of nanoseconds) X-ray pulses to provide the energy for exposure and the pulse duration for the exposure time of the captured image. These data are recorded on film with the use of intensifier screens to increase image density. X-ray films usually have lower spatial resolution than standard visible optical films. Multiple images of dynamic events require multiple pulses of X rays on the same film cassette or multiple pulsers each with its own film cassette. . . .

For two hours Garrett penciled furiously in a notebook, copying everything so he could study it again, and in the margin he noted questions to ask his father. There were still some fine points he didn't understand.

The dusky air had a bite as he navigated from his bus stop to home. From the sidewalk he could suddenly hear piano chords drifting out of the house. His father only played when he was relaxed and in a good mood. Garrett settled on the couch and watched as Clarence's fingers swept with power and authority over the keys. Garrett loved to listen, his father played with the same passion as when he talked about philosophy or economics.

When they sat down for dinner, Garrett mentioned how much he had read at the library. Patiently, Clarence fielded his questions about laser diode illumination, and temporal and spatial resolution of optical signals. He seemed pleased when Garrett opened his notebook and scribbled the answers.

"Guess what?" Garrett said when he finally put his notes away. He wanted to be modest, but he couldn't keep this to himself. "I'm going to be a starter tomorrow."

107

"There's a game?"

"At home. You knew that."

"And the coach picked you to start? That's terrific, Garrett. All your hard work has paid off."

"I hope so. I hope I don't screw up, not like I did in the first game."

Clarence finished his cake in silence. Garrett kept peeking up from his plate. Why didn't his father act more pleased, or give him the assurance he'd play well?

"Dad, you're coming tomorrow, aren't you?"

"I can be there," Clarence replied after a beat, "but I'm afraid you can't."

Garrett froze.

"You have to make a drop for me. Tomorrow afternoon. Precisely at four. It's crucial."

His foot drummed the floor. "You can't mean that—"

"We've had this discussion before. We've talked about the importance of our priorities. I thought you told me that you were sure you wanted to be a spy."

"Dad," he interrupted in a wobbly voice, "I've worked two months for this chance to start. I come home every day from practice black and blue. I deserve to start tomorrow. I want to start tomorrow. You're asking me to miss the game altogether? You were right about me missing the party, but this is different. Can't you let me off this once?"

"I'm asking you to honor the commitment you made. How can you brush off the importance of what you're doing? And what about the danger to my life? You said you would do anything to help me, didn't you? Is a football game more important?"

Garrett lolled his head back. His father's voice was in total control. This couldn't be happening. "What am I supposed to tell the coach?"

"I think it best to tell him nothing. You'll stay home from school tomorrow. Stomach flu. I'll write you a note for Monday. So you miss one game—"

"Now you're telling me to lie?" he protested.

108

"I'm telling you the end justifies the means. Apparently that's something you still have to learn, Garrett. I thought you were a student of history. Some of the world's greatest leaders have shown us that if a goal is worthwhile, so is any sacrifice to meet it."

Garrett's eyes closed in frustration. The confident, sober tone of his father rang in his head. He didn't want to hear anymore. Was this spy stuff for real, anyway? Was his father's life really in jeopardy? When he'd first agreed to help, Clarence had told him it wouldn't interfere with his life or his safety. If this wasn't interference, what was? Was he made of the same genes as his father? Did he want to spy for his country?

"Dad," he tried again, "I don't know if this is going to work out. You tell me it's okay to do what I want—you said you respected my independence, you told me to explore the city to my heart's content—but you never let me! You pull me away at every critical moment. I have to do something for you instead of something for me. I wouldn't mind if we took in a ball game or went to the beach, but we never do anything except stay in this house."

Clarence had risen from the table and padded toward the hall closet. He brought back the sleek, white electronic framing camera, the one he always took to Korea, and laid it carefully in Garrett's hands.

"It's time you learn to use this," he said. "That's what you've always wanted, isn't it?"

"I don't think I feel like it right now."

Clarence handed him a small flathead screwdriver. "This is an Imacon Seven-ninety. It costs two hundred thousand dollars and is more sensitive than a vial of nitroglycerin. Open the latch carefully, Garrett. I trust you. You can do it. I want you to see the guts of this thing."

Garrett realized his father was totally changing the subject and not dealing with what he'd just explained. He took the camera. The small screws came out one by one. Holding his breath, he removed the cover and stared at a maze of wires and tubes.

"Let's start with the film," Clarence began as if they hadn't had any words. "The camera uses a high-speed negative, like a Polaroid forty-seven, six-twelve, or six-sixty-seven. It goes right there, between the fiber-optic face plate and the imaging tube. Now, look in the viewfinder—"

"I know all this, Dad," Garrett said almost impatiently. "I know how the camera works. Light, either from the object you're photographing or from another source, like a flash X ray, enters through the lens. The camera takes this optical signal from the subject matter and passes it through that long tube we're looking at—it's called the imaging tube—which converts the optical signal into an electron beam. The electron beam, with the help of an oscillator, is fed to shutter plates, which deflect the beam across the slit in the aperture plate, giving two pictures for each complete cycle of the oscillator. To prevent vertical smearing of the images, a sine wave is fed to what's called compensating plates, which are near the shutter plates. The pictures are thereby positioned alternately above and below the center line of the film, like a split image."

"I'm impressed," Clarence said, standing back.

Garrett relaxed as he began closing up the camera. He was doing something right, at least. He knew he really enjoyed the cameras. Maybe he could do more than he'd imagined possible.

"Now that you understand the theory," Clarence continued, "the main trick in using the camera is knowing when to start and stop the shutter. We call that 'triggering.' It's a complicated and crucial timing process that involves photodiodes. Photodiodes are like sensors in the camera that read the light coming in and activate what's called staircase waveform; these control the electron beam. One of the most reliable trigger techniques is using a laser beam—the object you wish to photograph crosses that beam, which in turn activates the camera shutter. We can't do that without being in a lab, but I can still show you how the camera works."

110

Garrett watched as his father took the tripod from the closet, set it in front of the table lamp by the couch, and secured the camera on the tripod. He removed the shade from the lamp so the camera lens was pointed a foot from the bare bulb.

"Look into the viewfinder; make sure the lens is aimed at the bulb," Clarence instructed.

Garrett hunched behind the camera and squinted one eye. "Okay," he said.

"We're going to take a picture of a light bulb going on. The naked eye will notice nothing, of course, but if the photograph's successful, it will show us the actual path of electricity as it travels up and charges the filament wires. There's a standby mode on the camera's triggering device. A prepulse, which you'll activate on the camera just before I turn on the bulb, will start the oscillator. No horizontal deflection is applied, and frames are beamed repetitively at the first two image positions, but no images are formed until the first light is emitted from our light bulb. Depending on the inherent delay of the photodiode, either one or two frames are recorded before the first step. After the film is totally exposed, the camera stops itself automatically. Are you ready, Garrett?"

"I think so," he said. Clarence's words were starting to make sense. On a signal from his father, he pushed the button, and Clarence flicked the wall switch. The camera made absolutely no noise. He waited impatiently as his father walked over and opened the camera. Clarence held the negative up to natural light; it took a minute for the exposures to appear. Garrett was awed as his eyes passed from frame to frame.

"Incredible," he breathed, looking at his father. In ten sequential frames the white line of light inched up the spidery filament until the bulb was lit.

"You're impressed?" Clarence asked, smiling.

"It's magic. Can I try it again? Maybe on something else."

"Of course," Clarence agreed. "What do you have in mind?"

111

"I don't know. What else moves like lightning around here?"

Garrett was startled when his father reached into his briefcase and showed him a large black revolver.

"Where did you get that?"

"I've always had it, but lately I've been carrying it. If your life is in danger, you have to be prepared to protect yourself."

Garrett was uneasy about his father's words. Having a gun in the house made the danger seem very real and possible. In Arkansas his friends had had plenty of firearms, and Garrett had experience with a rifle from a hunting trip or two, but his mother had never allowed anything dangerous in their home. He watched as his father propped an old pillow at the end of the sofa, sticking two thick phone books in between. He dropped a cartridge into one of the chambers of the gun.

"This is a crude imitation of what I do in Korea, but at least you'll get the idea of how to photograph a bullet in flight."

Garrett moved behind the viewfinder and set the camera at the proper range. "What about noise, the neighbors?" Garrett thought to ask, but when he glanced up he saw his father had already attached a silencer to the muzzle.

Operating the camera seemed almost natural. He knew what buttons to push, what to expect. The quick thud from the revolver jolted him as the pillow coiled back into the couch. A small black hole was left in its center like a bull's-eye. His father let Garrett retrieve the film from the camera. The light of the room was insufficient, and the camera shutter had opened too soon, before the bullet had reached the pillow, but Garrett could see the projectile, its markings and shape, as if frozen in midair.

"That's fantastic," he whispered. "Can we do it one more time?"

It was after midnight before Garrett was willing to put the camera back in its case. They had fired the gun a half dozen times. He kissed his father good night and went to

112

his room. Books were scattered over his desk. So much homework still to do. He was suddenly worried and tired as he dropped into his chair and stared at his English assignment. His college applications were on a corner of the desk. His history paper on class economic differences wasn't quite finished. If he was going to stay home tomorrow, at least he'd have time to catch up.

He shut off the lights and dropped his head on his pillow without thinking about anything that had happened or what he'd face tomorrow.

Someone was pulling on his arm. Garrett flicked an eye open. The sky was still dark over the apple tree.

"Dad?" he said, looking up. His father's handsome face came slowly into focus. "What time is it? What's going on?"

"We need to talk, son."

Garrett rose with an effort and followed Clarence into the living room. A suitcase was next to the front door.

"Where are you going?"

His father poured two cups of coffee, and they sat in the living room. "It's back to Seoul for me, Garrett. I got a call after you went to bed last night. This time I might be gone longer. Three weeks at least."

"Three weeks?" His mouth opened. "Your company doesn't send you that long."

"My company has nothing to do with this. Officially, I'll be taking my vacation."

"What do you mean? What's so urgent?"

"My government contact feels the South Koreans are up to tricks we'd like to know about, sooner than later."

"You're taking the electronic camera?"

"Yes. But that doesn't mean you won't be busy," Clarence said, catching the disappointment in Garrett's face. "I'm going to be sending you photographs regularly. You'll continue to make your drops." His eyes burned with such a serious expression that Garrett paid complete attention. "I'm depending on you, Garrett, do you understand?

113

Starting today. The first package is on the dining table. Along with a letter of instructions, I left spending money. Take the car whenever you need it. And you can experiment with the cameras in the closet. I trust you completely. You won't let me down, will you?"

Garrett struggled to come awake and tried to put everything in perspective. He gulped his coffee. A taxi honked from the drive before he could think or ask any questions. "I won't let you down," he heard himself answer.

Garrett rubbed his eyes. He tried to push away his anxiety as he watched his father quickly gather papers into his briefcase. He hated feeling helpless. "Dad, will you be okay? Will you keep in touch by phone, too?"

"I can take care of myself, Garrett."

"I was just wondering," he said, somehow finding the courage at this early hour, "why you don't ever let me travel with you."

"I told you," his father answered in his calm, unwavering voice, "I need you here for now. There's important work to be done. I can't count on anyone but you. One day we'll travel—to Europe, Africa, the Middle East, every part of the world you ever wanted to see. I promise." He looked at Garrett. "Do you believe me?"

"I want to believe you," he said honestly.

"Why don't you go ahead and apply for your passport."

"Really?"

"Do it today."

Clarence came over and circled his arms around him. Garrett began to feel better, but the last thing he saw was his father slip the heavy black revolver into his suitcase.

17

The spider monkey cages were not far from the African elephants; then came exotic birds from South America, the polar bears that rarely emerged from their rock houses, ibex and chamois, and five skittish giraffes. Garrett ambled up the walking path under the crisp November sun, ignoring the crowds that never seemed to ebb, no matter what time he arrived at the zoo. Usually it was late afternoon. He tucked the newspaper inconspicuously under his arm. He'd made nine drops in three weeks, cutting football practice for most of them. He'd lost his position as starter and that really bothered him, but what could he do? He would get it back just as soon as Clarence returned.

He glanced at his watch now, marching ahead a few yards and turning to be sure no one was looking. In a garbage can he dropped his newspaper with the packet of photos wrapped inside.

He was always tempted to turn around. He was afraid a curious stranger might retrieve the parcel, or a maintenance man empty the garbage early. There was never any confirmation from his father or his government contact—how was Garrett to know if the drops were successful? But he never turned back. Those were Clarence's instructions. He had to assume everything was going perfectly, because he never heard otherwise.

He whistled softly as he left the zoo. With each drop his confidence blossomed. Sometimes, like today, he felt invulnerable. Was he not a true Master of the Universe? He wished he could tell Adam and Cleeb. They'd never be able to top this. This feeling of power lasted even longer than when he scored a touchdown. But he was so assured, he didn't need applause, cheers, or recognition. The secrecy and the bond he shared with his father made him feel superior to the whole world.

Garrett, you will be notified by the post office whenever a certified package arrives for you. . . . On the outside of the wrapping, in code, will be the date and time for the drop. . . . Do not bother to look at the photos; just wrap them in the front page of the day's Times*. . . . Be especially vigilant of Chou. Just because you don't see him doesn't mean he isn't around, or won't appear one day out of nowhere. . . .*

His father had then mentioned the code, the zoo, and the importance of leaving quickly after his business was done. To Garrett's great disappointment, there was little that was personal in the letter, although it was signed "Love, Dad." This was business. Garrett was surprised that the usual rule of varying the time and location of the drops was eliminated, but he was sure his father had his reasons. All that was left to worry about was Chou. And Garrett had begun to think, despite his father's warning, that Chou wasn't such a formidable enemy. Never once had the Asian tailed Garrett.

Mindful of his father's letter, however, he was never careless. Approaching the parking lot, he leaned his back against his car and had a final look.

Driving back to the house he wondered when his father would return. It was already late November. In the day's mail there was no new card from the post office, but a brown envelope carried an official U.S. seal. Was it from his father's government contact? His excitement ebbed when he pulled out his passport. He'd almost forgotten he'd applied. The photo looked so strange—he looked decidedly older, very stiff and serious, like someone on an important mission. Well, he was, wasn't he?

He was a spy. Sometimes he couldn't believe it. A simple boy from Arkansas helping the security of the U.S. government and the cause of world peace. Whenever he left for the post office, nothing mattered but making his drop. Not football or academics or applying to college. He had no outside expectations to meet, no worries. The moment was what counted, and it gave Garrett a feeling of control over his life he had never had before. It almost made up for his father's leaving them in Arkansas, and for his mother's death. No one could abandon him or let him down again, because no one knew what he was doing, except, of course, his father. Now, this private world belonged only to him and Clarence.

Garrett fixed himself a light dinner. Then, as usual, he took down the cameras from the closet.

"Who can relate the specific events leading to World War One?"

Bodies squirmed, throats cleared; eyes strayed to the clock. Mr. Fenton's erect figure perfectly bisected the blackboard. "Anyone," he said, "who was Archduke Ferdinand?"

Cleeb's hand shot in the air. "The archduke of Austria-Hungary," he spoke up. "He and his wife, Sophie, were assassinated by a student who lived in Serbia. That was on July 28, 1914. Austria-Hungary declared war on Serbia."

"Thank you." Mr. Fenton ambled to one side of the board. "What countries allied themselves with Serbia?" The teacher's eyes roamed over the class and stopped on Garrett. "Mr. Murchinson, can you enlighten us?"

"Yes, sir," he said automatically, but he hadn't heard

the question. He was traveling with his father through Europe, sightseeing in London, Paris, Venice.

"Can you enlighten us?" the teacher broke into his reverie. "The allies of Serbia—"

Garrett dropped his head forward. "Great Britain, sir," he guessed.

"Who else? There were twenty-four."

Garrett nodded blankly.

"This was your reading assignment from Monday, Mr. Murchinson."

He heard the disappointment in Mr. Fenton's voice. It was the third or fourth time Garrett had been singled out lately, and on each occasion he'd sunk a little lower in his seat, certainly sinking in Mr. Fenton's estimation. He'd gotten an A on his paper on class economic differences, but from there it had been all downhill. Not just Cleeb and Adam, but the whole class probably wondered what was wrong. Garrett was no longer bursting to tell them about his extracurricular activities, or his daydreams about him and his father. It was none of their business.

When the bell sounded he hurried out. He expected to feel embarrassed or guilty for screwing up again, but nothing registered. Why didn't he admit it to everyone, starting with himself—he didn't care that much about school anymore. He didn't feel there was much of a challenge. The only thing that still mattered was football. He hovered by his hall locker, pivoting quickly when the next bell rang. He was off campus before anyone would realize he was missing.

At home he found the mail had arrived early. A telegram from his father was buried in the middle. His father was safe, everything was fine. He'd be home within two days, arriving late at night. Garrett felt relieved, and excited. There was a card from the post office, too, promising a fresh package.

He was always careful when he stopped at the post office. He strolled around the lobby before he got in line,

118

trying to look casual. No conspicuous strangers eyed him back. He signed for the package and was out the door before he saw the wrapping had been damaged. The code for the time of the drop had been almost torn away. *Calm down,* he thought in the car. He could handle this.

He decided to open the package, and carefully removed the photos. There was no note inside. Garrett scribbled his own message and wrapped it, without the photos, in the front page of the day's *Times*. At the zoo he made his normal drop. His note had been brief, and smart, he thought with pride as he waited at home. The contact was to call Garrett at seven P.M., letting the phone ring once before hanging up, then repeating the procedure twice more. Garrett would then know to drop off the photos the next morning at ten. If the time wasn't convenient, the contact was to ring four times and leave his own note by five P.M. at the zoo the next day.

Restless, Garrett sat at Clarence's desk and studied the photos. Despite his father's instructions, he'd begun to think he had a right to be more involved in this operation. He was practically as much an agent as Clarence. This batch of photos was no longer of bullets trying to pierce metal. The frame sequences revealed what looked like the inside of a jet engine, the trajectory of some moving part. It was impossible to tell exactly what part, but two of the photos held his attention. In the background, there was a blurred image on the metal, like a manufacturer's stamp. He remembered the first photo he'd found in the hall closet, the one Clarence had taken back. But this likeness was clearer than the one from the streak camera.

He took the magnifying glass and held it to the photo. The image jumped out at him. He scrutinized the second photo with the same surprise. It wasn't a stamp, it was a flag. The United States flag. Garrett stretched back in his chair. Impossible. Why would his father be photographing a jet engine of his own country? It didn't make sense. There had to be some reason; something was going on that Clarence hadn't told him about. For a moment he felt a

119

shiver. Was his father hiding something from him on purpose? He couldn't believe that, not anymore.

The phone rang early that evening. Garrett grabbed the receiver before the first ring was over. No more silent communications. He had questions that couldn't wait.

"Hello, this is Garrett," he said without taking a breath.

There was a pause before Cleeb's surprised voice answered. "What's going on, Murchinson? You sound like . . . I don't know . . . like you're upset, or maybe you're mad at someone."

"I'm not mad at anyone," he said quickly. "Listen, I'm kind of busy now."

"You're always busy. Doing what?"

"Just busy, okay?"

"All right. I'll be quick. I wanted to give you the news, in case no one else had. When you didn't show up again for practice today, Enderbee blew his fuse. You're off the team."

"Big deal," Garrett said lightly, as if he didn't care. He knew he should have expected it, but it still hurt. He decided the sting would pass. He expected Cleeb to be gloating, but his friend sounded concerned, as if he wanted to help. He obviously was waiting to be given an explanation. Garrett didn't have anything to say except good-bye. He realized Cleeb was upset, but there was nothing more he could do.

When the phone rang exactly at seven Garrett interrupted on the first ring. The caller immediately clicked off. The second time, moments later, Garrett was too late again. With the third call he buried his frustration and let the entire ring elapse. The room fell silent. He would have to wait until tomorrow to ask his questions.

Garrett was at the zoo by nine-thirty, oblivious to the morning drizzle and the nip in the air. He didn't think he'd slept, and he was too upset to eat. The pigeons trailed him up the walking path, where he dropped the wrapped photos in the usual garbage can. Garrett did not vanish back to the parking lot. He lingered by one of the cages, and finally took a seat near the concession stand. This time as the crowd of visitors began to appear he was grateful for the camouflage.

He wondered how long he would have to wait. He would stay all day if necessary, into the night. He was totally confused when he spotted the thin, gaunt Asian. Garrett sat still. He watched him reach into the garbage can for the newspaper and slip the photos into his raincoat. The man disappeared into the crowd. Garrett couldn't move. He kept thinking that he hadn't really seen this. There was an explanation that eluded him. But he couldn't conceive of it as the shock and pain burned into him like a bullet, lodging so deep he wondered if it would ever come out.

18

"It was Chou! I watched the bastard with my own eyes! He picked up the photos, with a satisfied smile on his face. It's always been Chou, hasn't it—"

Garrett's fury choked off his words. His foot swung out and toppled Clarence's suitcase. He didn't care what his father thought or did about it. What had his father done to him?

"You betrayed me! You lied to me!" Garrett shouted when he had his breath back. "Yes, you're a spy. But not for *our* government. Not for the U.S.A. All the time you were spying for Chou, against South Korea, against the United States!"

Garrett turned, expecting something from his father, but all he saw was an empty, dispassionate face. Clarence sat stiffly on the couch. When he had opened the door Garrett hadn't given him one second. He'd accused him and dared him to find any explanation. What could his father possibly say? Garrett felt disgusted that there wasn't even a flicker of remorse or shame across the handsome face. It was set like a mask.

"So tell me, Dad. Chou's your good buddy, not me or Quentin? Have you two gotten together and had a few laughs behind my back? Do you dream up new ways to fool me, keep me in the dark?"

Clarence's eyes blinked. His mouth twitched. "You're very wrong." His voice was tired. "Chou is our mortal enemy."

"Sure he is," Garrett snapped back. "I have proof that you're a liar. I saw him with my own eyes. If you want to tell me differently, it had better be good, Dad. The way you concealed things from me. Don't you have a conscience? The lies you told. The cameras belong to our government? Sure they do. Obviously Chou gave them to you, didn't he? You were assigned by your agency from one aerospace company to another? I figured out what happened. When you were in Korea on company business years ago you were recruited. You've jumped from job to job whenever a supervisor or colleague has gotten too nosy. You said you kept secrets from your associates because it would be damaging if they knew you were a spy. You're right on that one, Dad. They couldn't know you were spying against *them*—"

Garrett's face burned when he thought about how he'd trusted his father. He'd forgiven him for all the years of abandonment. He'd believed he really loved him. "Shall I go on?" he asked bitterly.

"Sit down, Garrett." His father rose and with an effort picked up the toppled suitcase. The voice was weak, but somehow in control. "Let me start with a question, if I may. Have you ever concealed things from me?"

"Never," he shot back, barely sitting on the couch. He felt like walking out. But somewhere he wanted his father to have an explanation, even if he knew there couldn't possibly be one.

"Never?" Clarence echoed quietly. "When I returned from Korea the first time, you'd taken down the cameras from the closet, yet you were afraid to tell me."

"I did eventually, didn't I?"

"Your beer drinking?"

"The same. I told you later."

"How about that C you received on your English test?"

"I didn't think it was a big deal. Should I let you in on every disappointment in my life? You didn't care about my life until Mom died. Suddenly you want to know everything. Ha."

"What about what you and your friends talk about at school? Am I privy to any of that?"

"What are you getting at? Don't try to trick me again. I'm not stupid." Garrett resented being put on the defensive. It was his father who owed him explanations. "I have my privacy. I have certain rights. . . ."

"Rights? Perhaps. I'm not saying what you did was right or wrong; all I'm saying is you had your reasons for keeping things to yourself. And what about your friends? Do you conceal secrets from them?"

"Only what you and I are doing. Because you told me to. We're supposed to be helping our country. Tell me, Dad, do you have an excuse? Or are you going to deny everything?"

"I deny nothing, Garrett, because I have nothing to hide. I concealed the truth from you willingly, out of necessity, just as I gave Chou and the North Koreans information about the project my company and the South Koreans were working on, out of necessity."

"What necessity?"

"World peace," he replied. His stare seemed to go right through Garrett.

"World peace?" Garrett almost choked. "You expect me to believe that? Oh, wait," he said, the sarcasm flooding his voice. "The meetings you and Quentin attended—the ones on ending war. That's all supposed to tie in, huh? You're a confirmed pacifist, right?"

"Do you want to listen, or not?" Clarence asked, dropping onto the couch again. "Have you already judged and condemned me?"

Garrett fought back his anger and decided to give his father this last chance.

"Do you remember what I told you about Vietnam?" Clarence said. "I didn't tell you the specifics. Would you like to know the day-to-day horrors an indifferent and blind government can inflict on a whole nation? The United States is to blame for the misery to both it and Vietnam. I will never forget what I saw. I will never forget who was at fault."

"A lot of people might hate the government," Garrett replied, "including some Vietnam veterans like you, but they don't commit treason or become spies."

"Garrett, you know me as well as anyone does. I don't act impulsively. I believe in well-made plans. If I work against my country, don't you think I have intelligent and valid reasons? Don't you know by now I have serious values?"

"I thought I did," he said.

"I pride myself on being a student of history and world affairs, but isn't it obvious to anyone with half a brain what's happening? The North Koreans are hopelessly behind South Korea. Their economy, technology, resources—it's a pitiable little country where everything is held together by a police state. Despicable on every level."

"Then why are you helping them?"

"Because of their inherent paranoia and instability. Because the further behind the North Koreans fall, the more desperate they become. They fear, rightly, that a stronger South will become the aggressor against them. Look at their history. The two countries are mortal enemies. If I can help achieve anything close to a technological or military parity . . . if I can help square the balance of power between the two Koreas . . . the greater the chance for world peace."

Garrett thought back to the meeting he'd attended with Quentin and his father. That had seemed sincere. He couldn't doubt it. "I don't believe you," he said anyway.

"What don't you believe?"

"For one, your right to break the law."

"Our government does it all the time, Garrett. In the

name of world stability and peace, the CIA conspires to assassinate political leaders, incite riots, supply arms to illegal rebel armies. If I have the same ideals, why don't I, as a private citizen, have the same rights?"

Garrett stretched uncomfortably. His father always had a rational comeback. Garrett tried to find the words to retort and catch his father.

"Oh, I think, down deep, you do believe me," Clarence said, interpreting the silence. "What you find detestable is that I wasn't totally honest with you. You feel hurt, or maybe left out. That's your sense of betrayal, not for your country. Well, I couldn't tell you the truth, Garrett. Why doesn't the CIA admit to the things it does? Because everyone would be shocked. Nobody could see how the end justifies the means. People wouldn't want to believe it. Just like you wouldn't have wanted to believe I worked for the North Koreans. Confiding in you that I was a spy at all was enough of a shock."

Garrett stared back. He sat on his hands to keep them from shaking. "Would you ever have told me the whole truth, Dad? If I hadn't found out on my own? Or would you have kept using me?"

"That point is academic. I knew that sooner or later you *would* find out. That's your nature. You're smart, inquisitive, and you wanted to help me."

Garrett closed his eyes. Why couldn't he just wish this all away? He rose and walked to the window. "No matter what you say, Dad, something doesn't feel right. You've manipulated me. You don't have a conscience—"

"Conscience?" he echoed, almost with horror. "That's the whole point. Can't you see? I don't care about government laws if the future of our planet is in jeopardy. There are higher laws, moral laws. In my own small way I've done some good in this world. Can you say that for most people? Can you say it for yourself, Garrett? Do most people care about anything beyond their immediate personal needs? A new car, a big home, a vacation on the beach. . . . Materialism is a disease. Don't you agree?

126

What about your history paper on class struggle? I took the copy you gave me to Korea. It was a brilliant paper, and I know you're proud of it, too. I think you feel conflicted about your friends at Wilshire. At first you were attracted to their easy life-style, but something in you honestly resisted. I'm willing to bet you feel the same as I do. . . ."

"I feel a lot of things right now," Garrett said sharply, "but mostly that you're a hypocrite. You gave speeches about reaching my potential, striving for excellence. You set the same high standards for me as you did for yourself. You told me to study hard and get into the right college—but you never really let me! You made me work for you instead. You made me into a traitor. Now I'm off the football team, my grades are a disaster. . . ."

"Are you blaming me, Garrett? Didn't I say you had to establish priorities? What's more important—having a sense of moral purpose, or taking home some A's and B's on a piece of paper?" Garrett watched, puzzled, as his father's hand trailed to his side. His face was pale. "It was your choice to help me, Garrett. You're almost eighteen. You're old enough to be responsible for your actions. Maybe you could have worked harder and done both."

"I didn't choose to help you, not exactly." But he didn't answer that he wasn't sure how he was forced. He turned back to the window. The night sky was a moonless canopy that made him feel he and his father were the only two people in the world.

"Garrett, you have to clear your head. You have to put your mother's death and all your uncertainty behind you. Whose side are you on?"

"I'm going out," Garrett said. "I can't listen to another word from you. You're trying to confuse me. I need to get away."

"Where are you going?"

"None of your business."

"The FBI?"

"What do you mean? I don't know what I'll do."

"It would be a grave mistake to tell anyone anything. Especially the FBI."

"I'm going," he said again, reaching the door, but he couldn't make himself open it. He hadn't even thought of going to the authorities. He just didn't want to see his father anymore.

"Garrett, I need your help. I'm in more trouble than you know."

Something inside him made Garrett swing his head back and look at his father. Clarence had freed his hand from his side. Spreading through his shirt was a red stain. He took the shirt off, struggling with one hand. Garrett stared at the crude bandage that barely covered a stomach wound.

"Dad, you're hurt. . . ." He quickly helped his father to the car. "I'll take you to a hospital," he said as he drove. Garrett refused to ask questions. He didn't want to know anything. He left Clarence in the care of an emergency room doctor, handed over the car keys, and vanished into the night.

19

The hum of late-night traffic faded in and out of Garrett's consciousness. He was too depressed for sleep, too full of confusion and rage. He paced the cramped motel room, dropped on the bed, and paced some more. Even if his father was in jeopardy, he never wanted to see him again. Why should he? Who had abandoned whom, anyway? Did Clarence believe so strongly in world peace that he chose to break the law? Did he have that right without telling Garrett? Garrett didn't doubt that the high-speed photos were of help to the North Koreans, but were they enough to even the balance of power? Did his father really believe they were? Garrett didn't understand this underworld of spies. He didn't understand the enigma that was his father. What was true, and what wasn't? What was real, what was not?

He picked up the phone. Whom could he call? Surely not Monroe. He'd never believe any of it, or he'd just say bad things about Clarence. Then Cleeb. Cleeb was decent—he'd continued to try to be a friend—but was he capable of understanding what Garrett was facing? Most Wilshire kids didn't care about the real needs of the world; they focused on themselves and having nice things. Where did Garrett belong? He shared his father's ideals, didn't he? Why did he still think sometimes about having a new BMW or TV or stereo?

Garrett needed someone he could trust. Maybe Monroe was the one after all. Monroe was a good person. Monroe cared about him.

There was only one way out of the conflict, out of this whole nightmare.

His uncle answered on the first ring. Garrett had never been happier to hear a voice.

"Garrett, you sound like you're right next door," his uncle said cheerfully. "Are you back? It's past midnight."

"No, still in Los Angeles"—he rushed his words—"but I'm planning—"

"I know why you're calling. It's about money, isn't it?" he interrupted. "You couldn't sleep, you're so worried. I told you not to depend on your father. Well, not to worry. I just mailed you a fat check."

"I wasn't calling about money."

"The antiques business has never been better," Monroe boasted.

"Monroe—" Garrett felt disappointed. His uncle sounded almost as bad as the kids at Wilshire.

"I sold the last of the furniture from your house a few days ago—it was your own bed and desk, Garrett."

He stopped. "You sold my desk?"

"Why do you sound so surprised? That's what you wanted, wasn't it?"

He supposed it was. Those were his instructions to Monroe. He remembered leaving his room and thinking it was no longer recognizable without the furniture, and that it no longer mattered because he was going away. Now it did matter. Now he wanted everything back in place. He wanted it to be his again.

"How's the house?" Garrett asked. "Is that okay?"

"I don't know much about the family living there. They

130

must be happy, because they pay the rent and they just extended the lease for two years, with an option to purchase. Frankly, Garrett, it's hard to think of the property as belonging to Sis and you anymore."

Garrett dropped onto the bed. *Option to purchase? It's my house,* he thought.

"Garrett, are you there?"

"Do any of my old friends ask about me? Billy, Owen, Skate . . ." he said slowly.

"They're fine, I guess."

"You guess?" Garrett wished he'd taken the time to keep in touch with the guys he'd known all his life.

"To be honest, I haven't seen your old gang. They're in school, I'm in my shop. Without you around as a connection. . . ."

He didn't feel like talking anymore.

"Garrett, are you okay? Garrett—"

"I'm here," he managed.

"Are you still doing well in school? How's football?"

"Everything's fine, Monroe."

"And your dad, still traveling a lot?"

"Yeah."

"Garrett, what's wrong?" Monroe asked. "I know you. Your voice gets real small when things aren't right."

Garrett wished he had prepared himself. "Actually, I've got a problem," he spoke up. "That's why I called."

"What kind of problem?"

"Well, I have this friend, he's in some trouble. My dad's on the road, so I can't ask him what to do. My friend did something really stupid. He helped another boy steal some—some jewelry. He doesn't know what to do now. . . . I mean, do you think he should turn his friend in? Is he in trouble himself?"

"This is no friend," Monroe sputtered. "Garrett, how could you hang around people like that? Your mom raised you right—"

"I don't need a lecture," Garrett interrupted. "Just some advice I can pass on, okay?"

131

"Okay, son. Calm down. First thing I'd tell your friend is to never go near that other boy again. Would I turn him in? I don't know. . . . Your friend might be implicating himself."

"What do you mean? What if my friend has a good excuse?"

"Doesn't matter. In the eyes of the law he's guilty, too, just as surely as the boy he helped. He's an accessory."

Garrett's mouth had gone dry. "Monroe, I better go. It's late."

"Garrett, don't do anything foolish. If you've made a mistake, don't get in deeper."

"I told you, everything's fine with me."

"I sure hope so, son. Now, when are you coming to visit? I miss you Garrett."

"Soon," he promised. And said good-bye. He slumped back on the bed. What was there to go back to in Rainbow? He had no friends, no house. He wished now he'd never left Arkansas. He had done this to himself, he realized, but whom could he turn to to help him out of this mess?

He made the motel room his new home. He left only for food and an occasional walk. He was sure the right decision would come. He was surprised and almost angry at himself when he began to worry about his father. Who had shot him—Chou? Would he try again? Was that what Clarence was trying to tell him? Despite his bitterness, Garrett wondered how he could ignore his father totally if he was in danger.

On the third night he began to wonder if he could convince his father to turn himself in. Yes, that's what he would do. They would both be safe then. No one would have to worry about Chou anymore. The FBI would understand. Garrett would make them. His father hadn't betrayed his country for personal gain, not like the spies he read about in the newspaper. He believed in an ideal, and so did Garrett. That was something he was proud to have in common with his father. The authorities would have to take motive into account. The whole sorry matter would finally be over.

When he checked out of the motel on a bright, cool afternoon, it was as if a great burden had been lifted, as if he were flying. In less than an hour he was at his father's.

20

"I knew you'd come back, Garrett. I would have bet my life on it."

His father looked weak as he sat on the couch. The tired face fixed on Garrett. He had been gone only three days, but newspapers, magazines, books were scattered on the floor. The kitchen sink was piled high with dishes. It was as if his father had lost some control. Somehow that made Garrett feel better.

"You don't look well, Dad." Garrett stayed near the front door. "How long were you in the hospital?"

"They removed the bullet, cleaned the wound, and I was gone. I gave a false name so they won't come asking questions. Anyway, it's not important. Sit down, son." The clear, confident voice contradicted Clarence's appearance.

"No, Dad. I came here to tell you something."

"I'm listening."

Garrett summoned all his courage. "I want you to turn yourself in."

He was relieved to have gotten the words out. A thin

smile broke on Clarence's worn face. "Are you trying to save me, Garrett?"

He nodded. He wasn't going to be talked out of this.

"Sons have always done that with their fathers. I tried it with mine. I thought I knew more than he did. I certainly thought I knew what was best for him. I'd lecture him on his laziness and lack of purpose. He actually listened politely, drink in hand. Of course, he never changed an inch."

"This is different," Garrett said. "You're in serious trouble. This isn't a matter of being a drunk who won't put down the bottle. You broke the law."

"Have you considered the consequences of what my turning myself in will be?" Clarence interrupted. "You must turn yourself in, too. We're in this together. Don't think that because you're a minor you'll be treated as an innocent. You'll go to jail as surely as I will."

"There's such a thing as right and wrong." Garrett continued his argument, but the thought of prison stunned him as much as when Monroe had implied it. Garrett still thought he'd done nothing wrong. He wasn't thinking only about his motives. The truth was he hadn't known he was spying against his country. Would he really be put in jail?

"You shouldn't call the FBI, Garrett. Fear of the unknown aside, you're my son. We're flesh and blood. You didn't really come here to ask me to turn myself in. You came to see me and check that I was all right. Maybe you came expecting me to get *you* out of trouble."

"No," he said emphatically, trying to hide that his father had hit a nerve.

"Then why? You didn't come just to say hello and then leave. I know you won't abandon me, because you know yourself how painful it is to be abandoned."

"I came here to reason with you," he said. "I came to end this whole thing."

"I don't think so. You came to be reasoned with. To be

persuaded. You believe as much as I do in ending aggression and promoting world peace. If patriotism is in the eye of the beholder, so is committing espionage."

"You're missing the point." Garrett tried to present his logic coolly, but his heart had risen to his throat.

"The point," Clarence repeated, astonished, "is that my life is in danger. I was shot by Chou, who was at the airport to greet me. In the parking lot we argued over photos I was supposed to give him. I refused. I didn't have them. That's when he pulled his gun. If I'd been quicker, I would have shot him first. I managed to dress my own wound, and then I made it home. I haven't even been able to tell you—you never gave me a chance. If Chou doesn't get more photos from me, he'll be back with his gun."

"That's all the more reason to turn yourself in."

"You aren't listening. Clear your head. Outsiders can't save us. We have a crisis, and we have to deal with it ourselves. We will deal with it. Do you understand?"

"What I understand is we broke the law! We could go to jail. That's the point."

"We'll go to jail if we turn ourselves in. Think a little, why don't you? Don't let yourself be judged by someone else's yardstick. Haven't you learned anything from me? To the government we may be traitors, but I see it differently. The government is the traitor for doing nothing to keep this world from destroying itself."

"That sounds wonderful," Garrett said, suddenly fed up with his father's distorted logic. "Sure, set all the private standards we want. Let's believe in world peace and economic equality and all things wonderful. No matter how great your ideals, they're hollow, Dad. You know why? I don't think you like people—not your parents, my mom, your colleagues. You care about ideals but not about people." He hesitated. "I wonder if you even like me."

Had his father heard Garrett at all? Didn't anything register? His face looked blank. "I mean, Dad, isn't that why you never trusted me? Because you don't love me?

You say you do, but you don't really. You would never have told me the truth about who you were really spying on. As long as I helped you, that was all that mattered. You wouldn't hassle me if I failed at school because I'd be serving the greater good. And even if I figured it all out, like I did, you'd bet that I'd still accept it. I wouldn't mind betraying my country because I'd see the same justifications for it as you." He stopped, stunned at what he suddenly understood. "You think I'm just like you."

"Aren't you?" Clarence asked. "We both know what it means to be abandoned. We both need something to believe in. We need each other."

Garrett turned away. Maybe it was true. Maybe they were even more alike than he first realized. He just wondered if that was good or bad. He wondered if there were other implications.

"Why did you like making those drops? Being a spy?" His father's voice followed him. "Why are you so good at it? Admit it—you liked it—"

His stomach welled up with pain. He didn't turn around. "I only helped because I thought you were in danger," he said defensively. "Because I loved you."

"And now you don't? You can turn off your love, just like some faucet?"

"I'm not sure," he said, trying to get to the door.

"I'm still in danger, Garrett, and so are you. I can help you, but you have to help me first. Chou wants more photos. Our engineers have never tested the special alloy that's on the X Forty-four, not with weapons fire—we've let the South Koreans do that, up to now. But in the last month we've started the same tests here, to confirm the Koreans' results. Suppose someone came into the lab at night, when there's not much activity at the plant. . . . Everything could be set up to run all the weapons tests in the world. The cameras are there, and you know how to use them."

"This is crazy," Garrett whispered.

"Just a couple of nights in the lab, Garrett, and we'd

have enough new results for Chou. Then he'd be out of our lives. Isn't that what you said you wanted."

He turned, cocking his head. "For how long, Dad? Forty-eight hours?"

"No. This is our last time. I swear it. We're not helping Chou anymore. We'll disappear together. Garrett, you always wanted to travel. You have your passport now. We could take off for a much-deserved vacation, just the two of us."

Garrett clucked his tongue.

"We can make this happen, Garrett. New photos would give Chou definitive proof the alloy works. . . . Both the Americans and the South Koreans will have tested it. I know North Korean engineers are trying to produce the same metal—the more Chou can convince everyone of its advantages, the more money the North Koreans will devote to the project. This will make him a hero. He won't need to come after us anymore."

The idea was absurd. How did his father expect him to sneak into an aerospace plant that was guarded like the Pentagon?

"There's a way you can get in." Clarence spoke, reading his mind again.

He wiped his hands on his jeans. The room had turned unbearably warm.

"Remember when Chou took your voice print over the phone?"

"How could I forget?"

"That print has been fed into the computer that activates the lab room door."

"That's impossible. How could Chou get in—"

"He didn't. I did. I went into the lab myself, last night. Don't look so furious. I had no choice, Garrett. Chou threatened to kill us both, unless you help with the photos."

"You had no right. You figured I'd cave in and help you no matter what? How arrogant can you be?"

138

"I did what was necessary to survive, to help us both. How can you be so ungrateful, Garrett?"

Clarence pulled a laminated identification badge from his shirt pocket. Garrett knitted his brow at the color photograph. The somber face stared back at him. It was his extra passport photo.

"This is something else I did last night. I told you, Garrett, I try to anticipate all contingencies. The badge looks genuine, don't you think? More important, you look much older than seventeen or eighteen, especially with your hair combed back. You'll have no trouble getting past initial security. Once you put on a white smock and get to work in the lab, no one will be suspicious. It's as big as a city in there."

Garrett turned to the door again.

"I would do this myself," his father explained, "but I'm still weak. It almost killed me to drive to the lab last night. You want to talk about risks? What if we don't give Chou what he wants? Isn't that your ultimate fear, too?"

"I'm going, Dad," he whispered as he turned the knob. "You created this mess, you get yourself out of it."

"There's no way out, son."

"Yes, there is. Right through this door."

But when he moved outside into the cool, blustery December afternoon, he managed only a few blocks before he turned back.

21

"**G**arrett . . . Murchinson."

He had hesitated before speaking his surname into the metal box, and his voice had wobbled. The computer, however, detected nothing out of the ordinary. The door whooshed open as if Garrett walked through it every day. The long, narrow, windowless room stood empty, just as Clarence had promised, but it still felt like the whole world was watching him. Garrett slipped on a white smock from a hanger. He was careful to transfer his employee badge to the outer pocket, should someone wander in during the night. As he stepped into the corner lab with the viewing window, his watch read a quarter after midnight—he had almost six hours before the morning shift arrived.

He opened the laboratory locker identified by Clarence. The Imacon 790 high-speed framing camera was identical to the one at home. He hesitated as he lifted it out. Was he doing the right thing? As much anger and confusion as he felt, he could not make himself disappear when Clarence needed him. He had always been there for his mother. Of course, she'd always been there for him. What would she want him to do now? What would she say if she knew Clarence was a spy? And now he was a spy, too. But his mother was dead. All he had was his father, and his father was saying it was okay.

It wasn't really okay, and Garrett knew it. He was helping now, but he planned a surprise for his father. As exotic and enticing as a vacation in Europe or the Far East sounded, Garrett and Clarence were not going to go anyplace. Garrett had looked up the FBI in the phone book. There actually was a listing. He was almost surprised the FBI had an office in L.A. In a couple of days—just as soon as they were out of immediate danger —he would tell the authorities his story. Garrett would take his chances about being sent to jail. That was less of a risk than dealing with Chou, or breaking more laws.

He began to feel better as he adjusted the camera on its tripod, but something still nagged him. Was he really here just to save his father's life? His face prickled when he thought about the uncomfortable feeling deep inside. *He envied his father.* He envied Clarence's coolness and control. The world was caving in, but his father seemed to have some secret well of confidence. If they were so much alike, as his father had said, why didn't Garrett have that same control? He was afraid of taking any more risks with Chou, yet maybe he didn't take enough. Hadn't Cleeb and Adam been after the same thing with their Masters of the Universe game? True power, true control, came from not being afraid. His friends had been attracted to him because they said he was different. Was he really like his father? Did he have the same will to power? The stakes were great, and so was this test. Maybe by coming into the lab tonight he had confronted his fears of failure and overcome them.

Boxes of film were stacked in a nearby drawer, but Garrett had brought his own; his father had warned that the inventory was counted and monitored. He loaded a single unexposed print into the camera and aimed the lens at a long, low aluminum table with several pairs of

141

sturdy clamps at each end. From another locker he removed a fragment of the alloy the size of a dinner plate and secured it in one of the clamps. The metal was shiny brown and amazingly light. It was pitted with bullet marks from previous tests. A few more wouldn't be noticed.

Garrett's eyes glided to the corner closet where the high-power semiautomatic and automatic rifles were supposed to be kept. He spun the lock combination, and the door opened. The four types of rifles his father had described gleamed in front of him. From his jacket pocket he removed a dozen 5.6 M-193 cartridges that Clarence had bought at a gun store, and fit several rounds into the Italian Beretta AR-70 and an equal number into the French MAS. The American AR-15 and the German/Spanish CETBE 58.3 required a different caliber bullet, which they hadn't been able to find. He thought of his distaste for guns, but now he didn't mind as he secured the first two rifles in their respective clamps. He made sure the camera was in focus, set the framing rate for 100,000 fps, and activated the standby trigger to ensure a first-light recording. Donning safety glasses, he squatted behind the French MAS. As gently as he could, he squeezed the trigger.

The noise was like the crack of a whip. His shoulders coiled back. Garrett was sure, soundproof tiles or not, that someone had heard the rifle. What if a security guard came around? His stomach heaved as his eyes paraded back and forth. *You're panicking again,* he thought with disgust. He looked down to the end of the table. The size of a penny, a fresh dent adorned the metal. He removed the photo from the camera. The ten frames clearly revealed the bullet's trajectory and impact. *Beautiful,* he thought.

He scooped up the spent cartridge. His father had taught him the importance of paying attention to detail. He wanted to do the job right. He wanted perfection. On the back of the photo he wrote the type of weapon and bullet caliber, and slid it into his pocket before turning to the Beretta.

It was almost five A.M. when Garrett locked up the rifles and resecured the camera and piece of alloy in their respective lockers. He made sure everything in the lab was left as he'd found it. A sleepy security guard jutted out his chin as Garrett walked from the building to his car. The sky was still black, softening to gray at its corners. He kept the windows down as he drove the nearly empty freeways. He loved this time of morning when no one was around to hassle him. He felt free, loose, on top of the world.

Garrett had expected his father to be up and waiting for him to return safely. The house was dark when he parked in the drive. He found Clarence asleep on the sofa.

"Dad," he whispered, standing over him.

The eyes opened slowly. "Everything okay?" Clarence asked hoarsely. He struggled to a sitting position.

"Perfect." Garrett smiled proudly as he handed over the photos, but he began to worry when he turned on a light. Clarence looked pale and feverish. Days ago he had phoned his plant supervisor to say he was sick. Clarence refused to go to a doctor. He had managed to get out of the hospital once. He couldn't take any more chances.

"You did very well, Garrett. I'm proud of you." His father's breathing was labored. "I always knew you would come through. We're going to be fine. I've already started on our travel plans. Japan, Singapore, Hong Kong. I'll call Chou and arrange the drop—"

"These won't be enough," Garrett interrupted.

"You have over a dozen photos."

"I only tested two of the rifles. I think I should go back."

His father looked pleased. "You don't mind taking that chance?"

"The objective is to get away from Chou, isn't it? Let's give him everything we can and then be done with him. Dad, you look awful. Why don't you get some rest. I can handle this."

He wasn't sure why, but his spirits were elevated as he went to his room. He was taking another chance, wasn't

143

that it? His father wanted him to, so did he. He hated to admit that it gave him a high feeling. But he knew that soon the emotion and the incident would be history. He would be talking to the FBI within the week.

In the afternoon he found a specialty rifle store that sold the rare caliber bullets. He didn't have any trouble buying them. He was at the aerospace plant a few minutes before midnight. In the low-ceilinged room a stranger was hunched over a desk, but the thin, gray-haired employee only nodded pleasantly. Garrett slipped into the lab as if everything were fine. A couple more employees drifted in and out. For a moment Garrett wondered if they were security, maybe the FBI. He willed himself to calm his nerves as he set up the camera. He wasn't going to panic anymore.

He set his mind to business. The German/Spanish CETBE had a strong kick even in the clamps, and somehow the standby trigger on the camera didn't function properly. He made some adjustments. The second attempt was better. Still, the prints lacked clarity. His father had not been able to actually show him how to use a laser diode flash, but he had done enough reading, and he felt the confidence to try and make it happen. It took almost an hour before the flash went off. He substituted a more powerful lens on the camera, as well. Soon the prints were coming out crisp, sharp, flawless.

When he locked up the rifles it was after four A.M. The other employees had vanished. Garrett had over two dozen prints in his pocket. The night was an unqualified success. He made a careful inspection of the lab, stopping at one of the nearby desks and glancing through a thick manual. "EYES ONLY" was stenciled across the cover. Garrett skimmed the pages, but he understood some of the technical language about the X-44.

He drove to the beach to watch the sunrise. So peaceful. Maybe after all was said and done he was glad he had moved to California. As he sat on the beach feeling the fatigue of the last few days' stress, he saw himself walking on the ocean, floating toward the moon. Nothing could harm him. He was a Master of the Universe.

As he drove home, the heat, smog, and traffic began to bother him. He couldn't wait for night to come again.

Something smelled sweet and delicious when he walked in the house. His father, wearing his checkerboard apron, turned and faced Garrett from the kitchen. He looked unsteady on his feet, but Garrett's attention was mostly on what was in his hands.

"Let me light the candles," Clarence offered, putting down the cake on the dining table.

"Dad, what is this?"

"Happy eighteenth birthday, son."

"Happy birthday?"

"December 7—last time I checked, that was when you were born."

An embarrassed smile crept up Garrett's face. "I guess I've totally lost track of time."

"Sit down and blow out the candles."

"Thanks. This is a nice surprise, and a weird way to end a long day."

Clarence cut two slices, giving the fatter one to Garrett, and poured two glasses of milk. "To your success," his father toasted, raising his glass. "Did you really forget it was your birthday?"

"I've got other things on my mind, wouldn't you say?"

Garrett pulled out his night's work and told his father how he'd used the flash and experimented with several lenses. He was pleased that his father looked impressed. Why shouldn't he be? The photos were perfect beauties.

"I spoke with Chou," Clarence said. "You can deliver everything to him tonight."

Garrett thought a moment. "I still think it's too soon."

"You want me to delay the drop?" Clarence looked uncomfortable with the idea.

"That's what's been on my mind. How can we trust Chou? I mean, he shot you. What's he going to do to me if he's unhappy about something? And he always wants

145

more, doesn't he? I found a manual on the X-Forty-four. There're tons of information Chou would give his eyeteeth for. I can get it all. Security's not so tough at the plant. You know that. You got me in. And if you really want Chou off our backs—"

"You don't have to do so much, Garrett."

"I don't mind."

"Just remember, I can't stall forever," Clarence said, looking concerned.

"I need a few more days. Tell Chou I'm working hard. If he's a little bit patient, he'll really get important stuff."

"But I have to give him proof. At least drop off the photos you have. He needs to leave instructions about what he wants next. Tomorrow morning, after you finish in the lab, drive to a gas station on Sunset and Highland."

Garrett left for the plant a little before midnight. His mind kept spinning. He needed more time to figure out how to turn in his father. He had the phone number, but it seemed absurd to call up the FBI and announce, "My father's a spy." If he didn't submit proof, the FBI would think he was a crank. How could he convince them? Should he make copies of he photos? Would that be enough? He had to think this out.

Inside the lab room, he pored over a dozen manuals. They were technical, but he was able to interpret some information. On a yellow legal pad, as if he were doing a history paper, he made copious and neat notes. *Burner drag . . . thrust . . . centrifugal-flow compressors . . . axial-flow. . . .* He felt so sure of himself, he decided to look around. In a drawer in one room he discovered blueprints and several microfilm cassettes. Had his father lacked the courage to steal these things? Maybe Garrett was a smarter and more thorough spy than even his father. Maybe he was a natural. Some of the documents he copied on a machine; with the others he made additional notes. The microfilm he would have to deal with later, but he would find a way.

146

He found the gas station on Sunset without difficulty. Another cheap vinyl briefcase was waiting for him. Garrett didn't fiddle with the latches this time. He didn't care about the instructions inside; those were for his father. His challenge was working inside the aerospace plant. He would never be caught, he decided. He was too clever. He remembered how modest he used to be. He laughed at himself. Why should you feel modest when you were really good at something and outsmarting the world?

He parked by the beach for only a few minutes and watched the sunrise, but he wasn't relaxed enough to nap or take a walk. He didn't even leave the car. All he could think about was returning to the lab later to see what else he could take.

22

It was the day after Christmas when Garrett discovered a special room off the X-44 hangar. He and his father were still working out details about travel, and about Chou. Garrett had begun to feel so comfortable roaming the huge aerospace plant that he regularly opened and closed unmarked doors. If another employee happened to notice him, Garrett nodded smoothly and invented some colleague he was looking for. He was never questioned further. Garrett realized right away that finding this room was a real coup. There was a large, unlocked vault in one corner. Inside, hundreds of boxes, all marked "EYES ONLY" or "TOP SECRET," were piled on its shelves. He attributed the open door to some oversight, and was so glad to get access to the papers that even a week later, when the door was still open, he couldn't believe his luck. How sloppy could they be around here? The boxes were labeled with dates and subject matter. He almost laughed out loud because there was a copying machine in the next room.

He didn't know whether to be more pleased by his

audacity or by his stroke of luck. For over a month he'd been copying information from important but hardly sensitive manuals and delivering it to Chou, but this was the mother lode—the computer specs as well as blueprints for Air Force jet prototypes that looked like a fleet from Buck Rogers; technical information on radar jamming capabilities of the Navy; codes and code-breaking lists, including a cipher system called GY-22 and its keylist. . . . The treasure chest had no bottom.

The first time, Garrett copied only a handful of documents and secreted them in a backpack he'd started bringing. He had an attack of butterflies as he departed the plant, but the security guards knew him so well now that they didn't look twice. There was nothing to be afraid of.

"This is incredible," Clarence said that morning when Garrett showed him what he'd stolen.

"It was a cinch," Garrett bragged.

"Chou won't believe these documents. Can you get more?"

"I can get anything I want."

He went back to the special room every night for the next month and, day by day, copied over two thousand pages of what he considered the most crucial documents in the vault. Security might seem formidable at the plant, but it was really a joke. Walking in and out he was convinced he could steal the X-44 itself. He made deliveries to Chou weekly and faithfully brought home to his father the vinyl briefcase containing the Korean's future needs. It was all as easy as throwing a football.

He and his father didn't see much of one another, even though they lived in the same house. Clarence had taken a leave of absence from his job, and now he spent his time reading or cooking or playing the piano. Sometimes he took the car when Garrett returned and disappeared for the day. Garrett usually slept, or worked with his computer. His father had called the principal at Wilshire and said Garrett was transferring. It was so easy slipping between the cracks, hiding in the shadows. He didn't miss school;

149

life revolved around his nights at the plant. He still thought about when he would contact the FBI, but the date had become as indefinite as the exotic trips Clarence and he passingly discussed over dinner. Mostly they talked about Garrett's success at the plant and what Chou needed next. His father never suggested he stop, and Garrett wasn't ready to quit. Soon, he kept thinking, but he didn't know when. Just a little longer, until he'd given Chou more than he could handle.

One afternoon after he'd picked up the briefcase at the weekly rendezvous, he stopped at the post office to buy stamps for his father. He hated to wait in the long line. Fidgety, Garrett let his glance wander. On the nearby wall he noticed the eight-by-ten-inch cards framed in a crooked row. He stared. Some were yellowed and dog-eared, others were fresh. Above the photos of ten men and women were the capital letters MOST WANTED. One face of a young man looked no more than twenty. Garrett couldn't shift his gaze—if the facial structure had been slightly wider, the hair a little darker and shorter, that face might have been his.

He tried to calm himself. That could never be him. He was too smart to be caught, too good. He was better at the game of spying than his father, and Clarence had never been apprehended.

The line inched ahead. His pulse quickened in his wrists and throat. He had to get out of here, he thought. He opened and closed his fists. Why couldn't he move? Where was there to go? At night he went to the aerospace lab. His father no longer seemed the brilliant figure he'd made him out to be. Chou? His enemy didn't seem so dangerous now. He had nowhere to go. School didn't exist. He'd no friends left. Football was over, plans for college were never made. He occasionally called Monroe, but he tried to keep the conversations short and general.

His stomach tightened. Everything suddenly felt out of control. How was that possible? *He* was supposed to be in control.

Garrett stepped from the line, but his eyes couldn't leave the FBI most wanted poster. It hit him hard. He was never going to turn himself or his father in. He was never going to stop being a spy. This would go on forever. Just as it had for his father.

Maybe he and Clarence were exactly alike after all. That was what his father had always said and wanted. Garrett felt another chill. Wasn't that what he had wanted, too?

"Garrett . . . Garrett Murchinson!"

The deep voice boomed from behind. Garrett froze, waiting for a tap on the shoulder.

23

"It is you, isn't it, Garrett? You look pale—"

"Hi." He tried to sound casual, but he had barely caught his breath. The jowly, teddy-bear face and Santa Claus belly were poorly camouflaged by the loose-fitting suit. The trademark pipe protruded from the jacket pocket. Why wasn't Quentin Abbey in New York?

"Are you visiting?" Garrett thought to ask.

Quentin crinkled his brow. "Visiting?"

"You left the aerospace firm and moved to New York. You're a professor now, aren't you?"

"Who told you that?"

"Dad."

You got tired of being a spy, you were afraid of being caught, Garrett wanted to add, feeling superior suddenly, but he didn't say a word. Did Quentin know that Garrett knew he'd been a spy? Did he know his father had taken him into the spy game, too?

"What else did your father tell you?" Quentin asked in a serious voice.

Garrett thought of politely excusing himself, but something about Quentin's face made him curious.

"Yes, I left the aerospace firm," Quentin acknowledged. "But I didn't leave Los Angeles. I took a job as a science writer. I really enjoy it, which is more than I can say about my previous work."

What did Quentin mean by previous work? Garrett wondered. Both stood self-consciously, unable to look one another in the eye. Quentin was the first to break the silence.

"Garrett," he said quietly, "do you have time to take a walk?"

24

The sidewalk was congested with pedestrians and bicycles. Garrett watched as two boys on skateboards glided down the handicap ramp, arms extended like rudders, laughing. He tried to remember the last time he'd had fun like that. He walked with Quentin through a thicket of sycamore trees, feeling anxious and distrustful.

"I know what your real previous work was. You know that I'm involved now, don't you?" Garrett finally said.

"I guessed that when I saw your face." Quentin looked straight ahead.

"Are you surprised?"

"No. I think it was inevitable. I am rather disappointed. I'm sad for you."

"Look," he said, struggling, "you were a spy, too. Don't feel sad for me."

"I regret what I've done deeply," Quentin replied. "To be totally honest, it's not only betraying my country that hurts, it's my naivete, my stupidity. I can't believe I ever got involved. I regret it more than anything in my life."

"Then why haven't you gone to the FBI?"

"Believe me, I think about it often."

"But you haven't done anything."

"No," he said. "It's very hard to turn yourself in. You keep rationalizing that it doesn't matter. Nobody knows what you did, so nobody cares. You keep hoping this whole business will fade away, into oblivion, and you'll be set free. Free from your fears, from yourself."

"My case is different from yours," Garrett insisted, fighting off the discomfort from Quentin's words. "The issue for me isn't that I thought I did something wrong. The issue is I had to help my father. After you left him, he was all alone. I was the only one he could turn to. He was in trouble. Is it wrong to help someone in trouble?"

"You're rationalizing, Garrett. Just the way I used to do."

"No! My father really was in danger. Chou was pressing him. At the airport he and Dad got into an argument. Chou shot him—"

Quentin's eyes filled with concern. "Is Clarence all right?"

"He's still recuperating. He took a leave of absence from the plant."

"Chou is a cold-blooded bastard," Quentin said succinctly. "In the meantime, I presume, you've been doing your father's work for him."

"That's right. I'm good at it, too." Garrett was still feeling confused and defensive. As ashamed as Quentin made him feel, he still liked being a spy. It was impossible to explain. It had to do with his father and their relationship. Anyway, what did Quentin know about that? What business was it of his?

"I've done as professional a job as you," Garrett continued to boast. "Even if my father wasn't hurt, what I did was justifiable. The North Koreans may have a totalitarian government, but they need military parity with South Korea. It's a good and necessary cause."

"I used to believe that, too," Quentin said with a deep sigh. "Your father is very convincing."

"What's that mean?"

"I know you're more than competent at understanding high-speed photography—Clarence spotted your potential right away. And once your foot was in the door—well, your personality took over."

"You don't seem to understand," Garrett insisted, annoyed. "You left my father because you got scared. You couldn't take the pressure. I've hung in there. I can take anything," he bragged.

"You're right," Quentin admitted. "I was getting scared. And so was your father. His nerves were every bit as shot as mine."

"I don't think so. Maybe my father was tired, but he wasn't scared or afraid enough to quit."

"No, Garrett, you couldn't be more wrong. Your father doesn't show his stress—he's an expert at camouflage—but he wants out badly. We used to talk about it all the time. The question was always how to escape Chou's iron grasp. The bastard just wouldn't let us go. Whenever we suggested we wanted to stop, he threatened us with blackmail, or to kill us."

Quentin thrust his hands in his pockets. "I feel for you, Garrett. I know how hard it is to break away from Clarence. He's a charismatic person. And you're his son, after all. But I need to tell you something you should know for your own good. I almost feel guilty I didn't stop Clarence—I knew he'd use you."

"You knew what?" Garrett demanded. He suddenly felt a shiver. Everything was out of focus again. He felt incredibly alone. He remembered how he used to think that Quentin lived such an isolated life. It was he who was isolated now.

"When I first met your father at the Helsinki peace symposium," Quentin continued, "I found him more than a little intriguing. He was a strong, good-looking man full

156

of wit and energy. He was also extremely intelligent and could speak reasonably on any subject under the sun, especially world politics and current events. And the way he argued his points—he was spellbinding, a pied piper.

"He must have been a wonderful professor when he lived with you and your mother in Arkansas. Perhaps he never should have left academics. But your father has a stubborn side. He got into the aerospace industry when he didn't make full professor. Didn't he tell you? Maybe he never even told your mother. Oh, yes, he's had failures, too. After we became good friends I began to see how frustrated Clarence really was. He didn't like his employers. He always felt he had to prove something. He didn't like his fellow employees, either. He said no one at work ever gave him the recognition he deserved. He was overlooked for promotions. Others got credit for his ideas. No one understood his genius, his ideals, he complained to me bitterly. That's why he quit so many jobs. He never got the recognition and glory he thought he was due. The Department of Defense virtually controls the aerospace industry, and Clarence resented that, too. I know that after his Vietnam experience he genuinely didn't like the government, but maybe the dislike was partly a rationalization for the personal insults he felt at work."

Quentin paused to take the pipe from his pocket. It seemed to take a long time for him to light it. As uncomfortable as he felt, Garrett didn't want Quentin to stop. He wanted to hear everything.

"Despite your father's many talents, Garrett, he was filled with unhappiness, and it seemed to come mostly from within. There was a tension and agitation in him that I glimpsed from time to time but didn't really focus on. More riveting to me was your father's passion for world peace. One evening over drinks, after we'd begun to socialize, he told me that he'd started working for the North Koreans. I was shocked, of course. Yet over the next few months, as I met regularly with Clarence, he convinced me of his logic. He also persuaded me to help

157

him. We would be a wonderful team, he promised. If we truly believed in our ideals, we had to put them to work. We had to take risks. There was no other way to serve our consciences."

Quentin drew in thoughtfully on his pipe. "I believed him, Garrett. That's the bottom line. For almost seven years. At first I worked for a different aerospace company, but I gave Clarence my top-secret research, which he promptly delivered to Chou. I felt guilty after each disclosure, but your father played down my doubts and even made me feel noble. In serving the greater good, everything was justified. Then something happened that changed my mind."

Garrett tried not to anticipate. He knew he was going to be surprised. He wondered how badly.

"Your father lived in San Francisco at the time, Garrett. I remember sitting on his patio when the phone call came. It was from some distant relative. Clarence's father had suffered a stroke and wasn't expected to live. When he repeated the news there was no emotion on Clarence's face whatsoever. He told me he had never gotten along with his parents, that he didn't want to see his father. I felt you only get one set of parents, so I persuaded Clarence to go. If he didn't, I said, there would never be another chance for reconciliation.

"Your father returned three days later. His morale was definitely improved. He showed me an expensive diamond ring. It was his father's one valuable asset, and he'd given it to Clarence on his deathbed. A peace offering, your father told me, a gift of genuine love and forgiveness. I was touched, Garrett. I honestly believed him. I'd always believed that your father had never misled or lied to me. He lived simply and declared that he never liked material things. The ring represented to him emotional, not monetary, value. I would never have thought anything else. The following week I was at his house again. Your father was running an errand when the phone rang and I answered. It was the relative who'd called the week before. She said the ring to pay for the funeral had disappeared. The family wasn't well off, and that was the only asset to cover costs. Did Clarence know anything about it, because the ring was missing after he left."

"What are you saying?" Garrett interrupted. "My father took a ring from his dead father?"

"He stole that ring, Garrett. I saw it in his possession. There's no other explanation."

"But why would he take it?"

"I've asked myself that question many times. Maybe Clarence felt entitled to the ring. Perhaps it was a substitute for his father's love, something he'd been denied all his life. Maybe he'd always liked beautiful things and never told me."

"You never told my father that you knew?"

"As I'm sure you're aware, Clarence is very hard to confront. He can twist your words, and his own logic seems flawless. But I was deeply upset. I told your father he'd received another call from the relative. He laughed and said now that they had his number, they were trying to be friendly.

"This incident of deceit really bothered me," Quentin continued. "I started to rethink everything I knew about Clarence. Especially why we were helping the North Koreans. I'm sure he gave you the same arguments—if the CIA could break laws, why couldn't he? The end justifies the means. The true traitor is the one who doesn't serve his conscience.

"But I began to think, Garrett. The government is the government. Somebody has to make laws. Better good than bad, that's true. But you must have *some* kind of standard. You need a definition of right and wrong, even if you don't agree with it. If you ignore those standards, if you get involved in a world of deceit, you only end up deceiving yourself."

Garrett could see the regret in Quentin's eyes.

"I don't know when Chou started giving your father money," he added. "Maybe it was happening all along. I

159

do know that after I became suspicious, I began to notice new possessions in your father's house. They were always tasteful—artwork, antiques, sometimes a case of a rare wine. He always had a quick excuse for their origins, but I kept pressing him. Finally he admitted that he was getting paid. He said I would be paid, too, of course. He promised to arrange it. He assured me I was not to feel guilty. He was going to explain the entire thing to me. He'd been waiting for the right moment. This was compensation for our labor. There was nothing wrong with accepting money. Our ideals would still be intact, untouched—"

"You're making this up!" Garrett shot back. "My father would never take money. He despises what it does to people."

"Really? How do you think he afforded your tuition at Wilshire Academy? The computer in your room? How did he pay for your expensive presents every birthday and Christmas? If he's taken a leave from the plant now, how does he pay the bills? You saw the gifts he brought home from Korea. He's got lots more stashed away in a warehouse. Don't you ever notice how he just disappears every so often? He loves to shop, surround himself with beautiful things. He talks a good game, but he's a deprived boy who grew up to be a man who wants things he never dreamed he would possess. I'm sure your father and Chou had an argument over money. That's why he was shot."

Garrett tried to ignore the sick feeling sweeping over him. "When you left the aerospace firm," he asked haltingly, "did you give my father a present? A very nice oil painting?"

"I didn't give him anything, Garrett. I didn't even want to say good-bye. I was afraid he'd convince me to stay."

"No." Garrett could barely speak.

"I rationalized for as long as I could that even if we were being paid by Chou, that didn't undermine our original noble motive. Yet in my heart I knew the money ruined everything. I had sold out. I was being exploited

160

and manipulated. By Chou, by your father. As much as I loved Clarence, I was disgusted. You're being exploited, too, Garrett. Your father thinks you're just like him. He thinks you're going to grow as fond of money as he is. He tells you that materialism is a disease, and maybe it is, but it's infected him."

"I better go," was all Garrett could muster.

"You must see what's going on, or do you want to fool yourself?" Quentin asked almost impatiently. "I know this is painful. Try to understand what your father is doing. You haven't just taken my place, Garrett. That would be too easy, too obvious. Your father is far more organized than that, far more ambitious."

They stopped to face one another. Garrett felt the tears warm his cheeks.

"Why do you think your father asked you to come to Los Angeles? Your mother's death was the perfect excuse. It was serendipity for Clarence. It coincided with my announcement that I was quitting. He asked me to stay a little longer, out of friendship and loyalty, until he got things straightened out. Until he figured a way for him to get out of the trade, too."

As much as he wanted to flee, Garrett was immobilized.

"Garrett, you were brought to Los Angeles for a very explicit purpose. Your father had gotten used to the gifts and expensive life-style made possible by espionage. Clarence wanted out of the trade, but he didn't want to lose the benefits. You were the logical answer, the only answer. You were at a distinct disadvantage. You knew virtually nothing concrete about your father, except the limited things your mother told you. Clarence knew quite a lot about you. An innocent Alice had communicated with him over the years.

"I was told to encourage you myself, Garrett. Initially I thought I owed that to your father. I was so wrong, I did you such harm. I thought maybe Clarence was just toying with the idea. I honestly didn't know that he had already talked to Chou and had the transition approved. I learned that later. The break-in at your house was orchestrated. Chou knew the time you were to make that fake drop at the drive-in. Your seeing him in front of your house was meant to arouse your fear and give your father credibility.

"The spy work you did, the drops you made, working with the cameras, testing the alloy? None of that was really crucial to Chou. Oh, Clarence continued to get money for your efforts, but not because what you produced was valuable. Chou already knew about the alloy and its properties. The main purpose was to get you hooked on spying. He wanted to see how good you were, refine your skills, so that down the road you would give him something that was truly valuable."

Garrett couldn't stop his tears.

"I imagine you were very good, Garrett, just like your father. When Clarence got shot, that was a blessing in disguise, I see now. Everything worked out so perfectly for him, just as he was sure it would."

"You're not making sense. . . ." he said feebly.

"Did Clarence ask you to get your passport yet? He has big plans for you. He wants you to be the best spy in the world. Even better than he. You have to be. You're going to take his place."

25

His temples pounded like a drum. A dull ache started in his belly and exploded into his arms and legs. He couldn't breathe. With a screwdriver from the glove compartment he worked feverishly at the briefcase latches. One finally sprung open, then the other. His chest heaved out. The rows of bills were in even stacks with rubber bands neatly around them.

Garrett felt like he was dying, or was he dead already? He remembered the numbness. It was the same as when the policeman had called to tell him about his mother's car accident—that sharp, chiseled voice. At that time he thought it was the same feeling he'd had when Clarence had left him and his mother behind in Arkansas. Was it really possible to feel worse now? He saw himself falling through black, cold, endless space where nothing could stop his flight. The disgust and loathing he felt for his father were overwhelming as he stepped out of the car for air. He felt a pat on the shoulder and looked up to see Quentin turn and go.

Was Quentin a messenger who had come to save him?

Garrett wondered if there would ever be peace for either Quentin or himself. Only his father seemed to have peace. That was because Clarence had no conscience, no sense of obligation to anyone. He felt superior to the whole world. Garrett closed his eyes. Wasn't he his father's flesh and blood?

Numbly he steered the car onto the busy street. Weeks ago he had researched the location of the FBI building. He had imagined this scene a half dozen times, but now it felt different. He was really going to go to the authorities for a new reason. He was going to prove he was *not* like his father. He was his own person.

A fresh swell of hatred propelled him up the steps of the downtown federal building. The twenty-story glass-and-stone edifice dwarfed him. He swung the briefcase of money self-consciously in his hand as he told the clerk in the lobby he wanted to report an espionage crime. He couldn't believe the words came so easily. No bells or whistles went off. Garrett was directed to the tenth floor, the office at the end of the hall. Nothing was stenciled on the frosted glass door, and inside, a busy woman looked up with such impatience that Garrett wondered if he'd come to the right place.

He gathered his courage and said clearly, "I need to talk to someone right away. My father is a spy."

26

It was difficult keeping his concentration. He was in a small, windowless office, hunched over a microphone and tape recorder. Two FBI special agents sat across the table. Garrett regretted now he had not asked for an attorney. The agents had given him the choice—but he'd figured he'd just tell the truth and wouldn't need one. Honesty was what counted, getting the facts correct. His father had tried to teach him that facts weren't as important as ideals; they were an inconvenience, even an embarrassment, a means to an end. Garrott wanted to prove him wrong. The FBI would see that Garrett was innocent. His eyes, however, kept darting to the opened briefcase of money, as if it proved otherwise.

The agents had already examined the bills just as carefully as they now listened to his words. Occasionally they interrupted him with questions, making notes on their legal pads. He began to feel more vulnerable than he did courageous. What were they thinking? Did they believe him? The agent who looked the more stoical of the pair, Garrett guessed was in his thirties. He had thinning hair but was fit and trim, with earnest blue eyes and a black mustache that reminded Garrett of his father's. The other was slightly overweight and stayed slouched in his chair.

"More coffee?" the heavyset one, named Jerry, offered with a tic of a smile.

Garrett knew he'd been talking for almost two hours. *His first day in Los Angeles . . . visiting the aerospace plant with his father . . . learning about high-speed cameras . . . the first phone call from Chou . . . the first drop he'd made for Clarence. . . .* He wondered if he'd omitted anything as his hands wrapped around the cup of fresh coffee. He felt bad for informing on Quentin, too, but his father's friend had to know this was inevitable.

"Garrett, how much money did you take for yourself?" Jerry asked. He turned his chair around and straddled it backward, resting his chin on the back. "Starting with the first drop—"

"I told you, I didn't take any. I didn't even know there was money involved. Not until this morning, when I ran into Quentin."

"But if you had known, wouldn't you have wanted some?"

"No," he said.

"You told us earlier you'd bought yourself a new wardrobe. And you admired Cleeb's sports car. . . ."

The agents looked at one another. Jerry coughed into a fist. "Your father never mentioned financial rewards or incentives?"

"Never, not to me."

"Yet that's what motivated him."

"Yes. I believe that now. Maybe in the beginning he was idealistic, but in the end he compromised himself. He expected me to do the same. And maybe I was tempted." He thought of the world of his school, how envious he had been sometimes. "I was tempted, but I never gave in. I'm not like my father."

"Garrett," the other agent broke in, "you knew it was

166

wrong, what you did. You knew that spying was breaking the law."

"Yes."

"Why did you do it?"

"It gave me a good feeling."

The face furrowed. "What kind of feeling?"

"That I was in complete charge of my life. That I had total, absolute power."

"Just this feeling was enough to motivate you?"

"It didn't start that way. My father got me into it."

"How?"

He shrugged.

"Did he physically abuse you?"

Garrett twisted his head in disbelief.

"Did he ever hit you," Jerry elaborated, "or threaten to hit you—"

"No," Garrett answered. "He never even raised his voice."

"Did he abuse you in other ways—not feed you, for example, or not allow you any privacy, or punish you constantly. . . ."

"No, never. A couple times he even asked if I wanted out. I told him no."

"Tell me what threats he did use."

"I never felt threatened. He was strict with me, but he always had reasons for it. Reasons I believed."

"Did he promise you something for carrying out the drops? A reward that wasn't money?"

"In the end we talked about taking a vacation together, but neither of us was serious."

The two agents traded another glance. "Garrett," said Jerry, "did you do this for a cause? You mentioned you believed in the same ideals as your father."

"I still do. But I don't think they motivated me."

Jerry tucked his pencil behind his ear in frustration. "So what did?"

"I'm not a hundred percent sure. In the beginning I just wanted to please my father. I wanted him to be proud of me. I wanted to meet his expectations, his high standards.

It made me feel good when I did that. Then, suddenly, I was doing it for myself. I didn't want to stop. I felt like I could do anything."

"Garrett, you told us how much you hate your father. You've said it more than once. That's why you came here."

"But at the time I felt differently. I thought I loved him. Pleasing my father was the most important thing in the world to me. My mother died in a car accident. I never really knew my father. Then there we were together. I wanted him to love me."

"Enough to cloud your judgment? Enough to drop out of school, give up friends, football, plans for college?"

"Yes."

"We're trying to understand, Garrett. Are you sure he didn't manipulate or exploit you in some way?"

He let out a breath. "Psychologically."

"Psychologically," Jerry repeated sceptically.

How could he explain? He wasn't sure himself. He had never stood a chance against his father—he saw that now—even if Clarence had never physically abused or hurt or coerced him, not openly, not directly. Even when Garrett had understood what Clarence was doing to his head, he had still been powerless to stop it. There were subtle things his father had said and done that Garrett was afraid he would always feel trapped by. Maybe that was the second scariest thing.

The scariest, he knew, was that his father had done this at all.

"Garrett, by your own admission, without coercion, you've knowingly committed treason against the United States government." Jerry's words broke into his thoughts.

"Yes."

The other agent motioned for Garrett to stand and place his hands behind his back. The cold steel wrapped around his wrists.

"I'm going to have your confession transcribed, then ask you to read and sign it. I'll call the federal public defender's office. In the meantime you'll be in lockup at the federal detention center. It's not far from here."

No, that's impossible. I'm innocent, he wanted to tell them, but he couldn't make himself say it. Maybe he wasn't innocent, not in the eyes of the law. The FBI didn't see into his heart and mind.

"Aren't you going to arrest my father?" he asked as he was led into the hallway.

"We're on our way. He's expecting you at the house?"

"He's waiting for his money."

"Maybe I can give you a break, if you want to just see your father, before you're locked up. I can't let you two talk," Jerry said, "but you could come with us."

He tried to keep the passion out of his voice, but he could hear it anyway, "I never, ever want to see him for the rest of my life."

.

27

"**H**ello. My name is Eleanor Hartmann."

Garrett slipped off his wafer-thin mattress as the guard let the woman into his cell. What was happening? It was Monroe whom Garrett was expecting. He had called his uncle from the FBI building, and Monroe had promised to catch the first plane to Los Angeles. He was shocked, but he said no matter what, he'd be there for Garrett. He cursed himself for ever letting Garrett go to his father. Across the narrow aisle, prisoners sat or stood or paced in their cells, glancing up at the attractive woman visitor. Garrett felt humiliated in his baggy orange prison jumpsuit.

"You're Garrett Murchinson?" the woman confirmed in a brisk but pleasant voice. She extended a friendly hand.

"Garrett *Woolsey*," he said pointedly.

"Mr. Woolsey, is it? Very well. Why don't you call me Eleanor. I'm from the federal public defender's office." She took the only chair in the cell. Garrett dropped back on his bed.

The brown pinstripe business suit and high heels made her seem slightly remote, but her face was soft and patient. She was short and slim. Probably thirty-five. The alert green eyes were determined. Her thick black hair was especially pretty. Garrett found himself taking in every detail.

"Unfortunately, this won't be a long visit," she apologized as she settled her briefcase at her feet. Her fingers pulled out a thick folder. "But the news I have isn't all bad. First, how are you doing, Garrett?"

"All right," he said, even though it wasn't true. He'd been in the detention center over twenty-four hours, but he couldn't make himself eat and he had barely slept.

"Are you really my attorney?" he asked.

"Of course."

"What does that mean?"

"That I provide you the best legal representation I can. I've been in the federal public defender's office for nine years. I'm good at my job. From everything I've read about you, Garrett, I think I can help."

There was something caring and hopeful about the woman that he liked. It was difficult peeling his eyes away.

"I read your confession thoroughly. So did several of my associates," Eleanor continued. "Garrett, is there anything you want to say, in confidence now, that you haven't already?"

He arched his neck, thinking. "I told the FBI everything."

"Everything you knew."

"Yes."

"The reality is you didn't know very much, I'm afraid. While you did some damage by giving Chou the documents from the aerospace plant, your information was mostly obsolete. That's going to be one of the points I raise in my letter to the U.S. attorney. You were just a pawn."

"No," he said defensively. "I knew a lot. I knew everything my father knew and more."

"I'm sorry. Not by a long shot."

She flipped through several pages in his file. "Chou Do Li," she read without glancing up, "has been under

171

surveillance by the FBI and the State Department for almost five years. The North Koreans have been on a desperate hunt for technology and military hardware, and Chou is the reputed mastermind."

Eleanor's eyes flicked up. "Chou was the reputed brain, but no one had proof, not until you brought in the briefcase of cash, Garrett. The FBI has traced some of the bills to a European bank where Chou has a large account. Your father has been arrested; so has Quentin Abbey. Only they're not talking—your father because he refuses, Mr. Abbey on the advice of his counsel. But the FBI is convinced your father was one of Chou's main pipelines for information. He's done far more than supply high-speed photographs of tests on top-secret weapons and planes. Over the decade, at different companies, Clarence Murchinson had access to code-breaking devices, eyes-only reports from intelligence sources worldwide, transmittals from the Pentagon. At one of his employers', someone fabricated bills of lading and actually got weapons sent to North Korea. That was probably your father." Eleanor put away the file. "Are you surprised, Garrett?"

No, he thought, ignoring the sickening feeling he knew so well. *Not anymore. There were no more surprises.*

"There's a small irony," Eleanor pointed out. "As much damage to national security as your father apparently did, he certainly wasn't Chou's only source of information. The North Koreans have become more adept at recruiting than the Russians. There's evidence that Chou has a European network more extensive than the one in the United States. When you view the whole picture, your father was little more than a pawn, too."

A cog in the wheel, Garrett remembered, just like Clarence was always afraid he was. *Just like I am*, Garrett thought.

"What this comes down to," Eleanor continued, "is we have one chance, Garrett, and one chance only." She threw back her shoulders, looking more earnest. "You have to give me a decision very quickly, if we're to have any leverage with the U.S. attorney's office."

172

"What leverage?"

"Because your father refuses to incriminate himself, it's up to you to build a case against him. You're an invaluable witness. You're the only witness. So far, Mr. Abbey's attorney has said his client won't testify. Are you familiar with the term 'turning state's evidence'? It means when a defendant agrees to help the other side, the prosecution—you make a deal."

"I don't understand. Either you're on one side or the other, aren't you? Why isn't anything ever clear?"

"It's how the system works. If you're willing to testify, I can ask immunity for you. I might well get it. If I don't, and your case goes to trial, I'll try to convince the U.S. attorney to file a sentencing memorandum with the judge asking to dismiss the charges against you. I can't give guarantees, but I know that if you cooperate—"

"Testify against my father?" Why hadn't he anticipated this? "Listen. I turned him in. You really expect me to go into a court and testify, too?"

"Garrett"—he heard the understanding tone in her voice—"I know this must be hard. I'm going to ask you to try to be objective. Here are the facts: Your father used you without the slightest remorse. Cold-bloodedly he persuaded you to be part of his terrible crime. He treated you like you weren't a human being, much less his own son. Don't lose sight of this—"

"Stop it, please," he interrupted her.

"I'm sorry. You've told everyone you hate your father. He disgusts you. Right?"

"That's the whole point," he explained. "I do hate him. I don't want anything to do with him, ever." Garrett rose and walked toward the front of his cell.

"Where is my father now?" he asked suddenly. "He's here, in this jail, too? Isn't he? Somewhere in this building. . . ."

"He and Quentin are in separate cells on the floor above. If you see your father in the exercise yard, will you pretend you're total strangers? That's not what you

173

need to worry about. We've got to get you to choose your best defense."

"As far as I'm concerned, my father doesn't exist," he said.

"That's not a reasonable choice for you at this point. Is that why you won't testify against him?" Eleanor argued. "What about your future? Do you want to spend the next ten or fifteen years in jail? Do you want the whole world thinking you betrayed your country?"

"I don't care about the rest of the world."

"Yes, you do. Garrett, promise me you'll think about this."

"I'm not making any more promises, not to anybody." *You don't understand, you can't, he's not your father*, Garrett wanted to yell at Eleanor. He perched on his bed, head bowed, paralyzed.

Eleanor snapped shut her briefcase and called the guard. "Please don't leave me," Garrett whispered. Eleanor caught him looking at her, but she didn't hear his plea.

"What, Garrett?" she asked.

"Nothing," he said turning away.

He didn't sleep well that night, despite his fatigue. There were too many things to consider—so many things had happened since he'd moved to Los Angeles—but finally he knew exactly what to do. He hoped he had the courage.

28

"I want to see my father."

Eleanor swung her briefcase from one hand to the other. She had just entered the cell, and she placed her morning coffee on the chair. His words had taken her by surprise. "That was a quick turnaround," she managed. "Yesterday you didn't care—"

"I want to see him right now, if that's possible."

"Garrett," she spoke deliberately, "you know that I want you to testify against your father, but talking with him ahead of time would be highly irregular. I know what the U.S. attorney's office would say—you and your father could communicate something that would undermine the prosecution's case. Or you could be threatened by your father, talked out of testifying. I'm sorry, I don't approve— and anyway, I doubt I could arrange it. The system doesn't allow this."

"Tell the U.S. attorney's office that if it wants me to testify," he answered curtly, "it had better let me see my father."

"Why?"

"Tell them it's personal."

Eleanor frowned. She pushed the hair from her eyes with a delicate flick of her hand. "Are you sure you know what you're doing? I hardly know you, Garrett. But last night I sat up worrying about you. You look as if you haven't slept in a month. The guard says you're not eating—"

"That's not relevant," he said quietly, but he was almost touched by her concern. "You have to trust me about my father," he said. "Please, just arrange this and I'll do what has to be done."

A guard came shortly before noon. He ushered Garrett down two flights of stairs and into a small room to the visitors center. Eleanor was waiting.

"The U.S. attorney's office gave its approval, reluctantly," Eleanor said. Garrett saw she didn't look happy. "With the condition that a corrections officer remain in the room. Your visit can't exceed three minutes. Is that agreed?"

"Agreed."

"Are you sure you want to do this?"

"Sure," he whispered. He clucked his tongue.

"Would you like me to accompany you?"

"I'd like to see you afterward," he said. He fixed on her smile.

"I'll be waiting," Eleanor assured him.

A tattered card table with two chairs anchored the room. Garrett took a seat with his back to the door, nearest a high window that permitted a sliver of natural light. The middle-aged guard pushed back his cap. He looked bored standing in the corner.

When the door opened Garrett didn't turn. He almost didn't hear his father's usual ghostlike steps. A shadow fell across the table. As his eyes leveled up, Garrett couldn't believe his father was smiling as he took a seat, as if he hadn't a worry or doubt in the world.

"Garrett, you don't know how good it is to see you!" Clarence's large, sure hands reached out across the table

176

and wrapped around his. The deep, sonorous voice was clear as water. As if nothing had ever gone wrong between them. "You don't know how relieved I was when I heard you wanted to see me," Clarence said. "Are they treating you all right? Do you need anything?"

"Stop," Garrett interrupted. "I'm fine."

"Did you know that our story is in all the media? Someone slipped me a newspaper. We're on the front page of the *Times*! Can you imagine? We're celebrities. As famous as any movie star! You know what I'm going to do? I want to hold a press conference. I'm going to reach the whole world with my message—I'm going to prove our innocent intentions—"

"I need to tell you something," Garrett interrupted him again.

"About what you did? Turning me in? Violating our trust?" Clarence leaned closer, bigger than life, his hands still encircling Garrett's. "I think you must regret that, getting us in trouble. But I'll find a way out. I forgive you. You've made mistakes before, but I always have the answer. You've come to me for help again, haven't you?"

His stomach began to churn. His father seemed as confident as ever, radiating an energy that sapped Garrett's.

"Dad"—he was almost surprised he could still call him that—"you're wrong this time. I am not sorry for turning you in. I have no regrets, not one. None at all. Do you understand? I want to tell you, face-to-face, that I'm going to testify against you in court. I'm going to be the one to convict you. With my testimony they'll send you to jail for thirty years."

"Garrett, that's a major decision you're making without much thought. I don't think you mean it."

"I've made it. You won't talk me out of it. You and your words don't control me anymore."

"What you're making, Garrett," came the unwavering voice, "is a mistake. You won't testify against me. You can't. You're my son."

"You say that like there's some law—"

177

"It's an unwritten one. You think a son can betray a father?"

"You're such a hypocrite. If I wasn't so miserable, I'd laugh. I'm supposed to love you, so I can't turn against you? Is that it? What did you do to me? Now and when you walked out when I was a kid. I have a responsibility that's more important than any emotion I might have felt for you. Guess what? I'm eighteen. Society expects me to be responsible. You said so yourself. I interpret that to mean there're laws, you and I are accountable—"

"You really believe that? About laws? After all that I taught you?"

"Yes."

"Then why did you ask to see me here? There's doubt in you, Garrett. I see it."

"I'm going to tell the jury everything I know," Garrett said firmly. "I'm going to tell them how I thought my father was a great idealist. The jurors are going to find out what you did to me—that you're the most cynical, hypocritical man on earth."

Clarence didn't blink. "Quentin won't testify against me. He's too afraid. What makes you think you have such courage?"

Garrett tried to withdraw his hands, but Clarence tightened his grip.

"You'll never do it, Garrett. You'll freeze. You have too many doubts, just like Quentin. You may think you hate me, but you really don't. You're afraid to hate me. We're flesh and blood. You don't have the nerve to betray me twice. In your heart you know it was wrong the first time. The second, you couldn't live with yourself."

"Oh, I'll live with myself," he said quietly. "It's the only way I'll be able to live with myself. I'm not testifying against my father. I couldn't. Because I don't know who my father is. Clarence Murchinson is an enigma. He's a man with all these layers. Every time I peel one back, I find another, and another, and another. I wonder if you even know yourself. All I can be sure of is you shut me

178

out of your life, just like your parents shut you out of theirs. You used me when you needed something for you. I was just a means to your tragic end."

"Garrett, you're deluding yourself! You're looking for an excuse to turn cold and unforgiving. You're not listening to your heart!"

Garrett smiled. For the first time he thought he could hear real panic in his father. Who had control now? "Dad, don't you really understand why I wanted to see you?" he said calmly. "I wanted to make sure I wouldn't lose my courage at the trial. I was afraid that as much as I despised you, I would look at you in the courtroom and feel the guilt you want me to feel, or some kind of strange loyalty, in spite of everything you've done to me. Can you imagine? This false bond you made me believe existed between us—I was afraid it could never be broken."

"Garrett, if you don't save me, who will? Do I have to beg? I need you!"

When he went to pull his hands away this time, Clarence couldn't stop him.

29

Eleanor was waiting outside the door. "I'm okay," Garrett said before she could ask. He tried to smile but it broke in the middle.

"Did you accomplish what you wanted?" She looked worried. "Your hands are shaking."

Garrett tried in vain to control the trembling. How could he deny that for all his bravery in standing up to his father, he was a wreck. Despite his hatred for Clarence, he felt like grieving all over again. He no longer had a father. For a while he'd had one, so he'd thought, but that had been taken away from him. Garrett wondered if he'd ever understand why Clarence had done this. He knew he'd probably spend the rest of his life trying to figure it out.

But there was a positive side. He wasn't the same person who had come to Los Angeles so wide-eyed and green. He had stood up to his father and shown his own values and worth. Maybe he had the confidence to handle any crisis now. Somehow he would see himself through the dark days ahead.

"I want to thank you, Eleanor," Garrett said.

"For what? I tried to stop your meeting. What exactly happened?"

Garrett bit down on his lip. "You remind me of somebody. That's what gave me the extra courage I needed."

Eleanor looked pleased. "Who would that be?" she asked.

"Are you married?" he said. "Do you have kids?"

"I'm divorced," Eleanor explained. She looked perplexed. "No kids. Sometimes I'm sorry about that. Why do you ask?"

"You remind me of my mother. You seem a lot like her."

Her face reddened. "I do?"

"I noticed it when we first met. You look a little bit like her, but mostly it's your spirit and kindness. You care about people. Obviously you care about principles, too, but people come first. My mom was like that."

"What happened to your mother?"

"I thought you knew. I told the FBI. She was killed in an auto accident."

"Oh, I'm so sorry."

He smiled painfully. "I'm getting over it. I have no choice, do I? I had other choices. I'm getting over a lot of things."

"I'm sure she was a good mother to you. I'm sure she loved her son."

"Yeah," he said, "I think you two would have been friends."

She circled an arm around Garrett. "I've got some good news. Your uncle's waiting next door, in the visitors center. We can talk about what you want me to do for your case after you see him."

"Family," Garrett said with a soft smile, surprised the word came off his lips. All at once it seemed like the greatest thing in the world. Flesh and blood counted when both people cared. He suddenly realized he had an appetite for food again. Maybe that was another good sign.

ABOUT THE AUTHOR

Michael French is a native of Los Angeles who currently lives in Santa Fe, New Mexico, with his wife and their two children. Time permitting, he is a serious mountain trekker who favors exotic and remote destinations, among them New Guinea, the Amazon, Java, and Rwanda. Michael French is the author of several adult books, as well as six young adult novels: *Lifeguards Only Beyond This Point, The Throwing Season, Pursuit,* which won the California Young Readers Medal, as well as the Starfire novels *Us Against Them, Circle of Revenge,* and *Soldier Boy.*